LIN'S CHALLENGE

INTERGALACTIC OFFICERS BOOK 1

MARA JAYE

LIN

THIS JOKE STOPPED BEING FUNNY THE MOMENT IT
started.

I woke up several minutes ago, I guess, in a dark gray
warehouse type of room. Fluorescent lights stabbed my
eyes when I opened them, so I listened for a while to get
my bearings. Men were yelling, and a couple of the women
were crying in the crowded room. Where the hell was I?
Then it hit me. I was either dreaming or was passed out in
a club at closing time. People lose their shit at three a.m.
when floodlights ruin their alcohol haze.

I propped up on my elbows and opened my eyes a
little. I saw people lined up against the walls, banging on
metal and screaming. Smoke wasn't lingering in the air, so
the panic seemed way off even for a dream. I also don't go
clubbing in my favorite cotton pajamas. Had I passed out
at a costume party, maybe? I didn't know and couldn't
make my brain work to remember, either. All of this was

too much input on too little coffee. I stifled a yawn and blinked the sleep from my eyes a little more.

Several others lay around me, unconscious. One guy moaned, but most were snoozing during the ruckus. Nice for them because now that I was awake, the noise was deafening. Even worse was how my sense of smell worked too well. I've never caught anything like the current stink in a dream before now. Since this is real, obviously, I suspect my boyfriend's at the bottom of it. Rick is just the type of guy to slip me a sleeping pill and coax his buddies into playing a prank on me. I love and hate him sometimes.

Time to end this little stunt, so I stand, or try to with wobbly legs. My last workout didn't seem so intense to leave my legs mush like this. My calves and quads ache as if I've been hit with a baseball bat. I look down, even lifting my capri-length pajama bottoms to check out my knees and calves. No bruises there or on my upper arms when I raise the sleeves, but still. If those assholes tripped and dropped me on the way here, I'll kill all of them. Or fix a choco-laxative batch of brownies served with a smile.

My legs wobble again. I really need coffee right now and blink a few times to clear the sleep from my eyes. After a closer look, all of the people here are either bulky men or gym-buffed women. Most of them are taller than most pro basketball players, too. Weird. We've lived together long enough. You'd think I'd know Rick had so many beefcake friends.

I make my way by stepping around some of the sleepers to where most of the others are banging on a wall.

After tapping one of the men on the shoulder, I smile as he turns around. His cat eyes take me by surprise at first. He's a little overly furry in the face. Kind of like his testosterone went haywire. But, working at a grocery store during the graveyard shift, I've seen all kinds.

He's actually clean cut compared to some of the heavily pierced types I work with. So, I give him my best smile. "Hello, we've not met. I'm Rick's girlfriend, Lindsey. Lin for short. Who are you?"

He shakes his head and says something foreign with purrs or rumbles. Turning away from me, he steps between a couple of other guys and joins in banging on the wall with his furry fist. The noise hurts my ears and makes a hangover seem mild. I'm not putting up with any more of Rick's shit. Especially not from some person pretending to be a cat. "Hey! Come back here and tell me what's going on."

Someone pushes me out of the way to get closer to the wall. Assholes. I'm this close to moving out and telling Rick he can shove our relationship.

I turn to look for anyone who isn't doing his or her best freaking-out act. A couple of Amazonian gals are standing in a corner, hugging and crying. Ug. Not going there for the fake tears. A couple of the formerly unconscious ones are sitting up and looking around. They're doing a good job of acting. I'd be impressed if this weren't a huge pain in the ass.

A loud whistle like the one people do at ball games rings out. As if the usual cacophony wasn't enough, right?

But it works. Everyone stops cold, and then a calm female voice begins speaking over an intercom I can't see.

And...I have no idea what she's saying. I'm fluent in English and have a tourist level of German. This doesn't even sound like Cat Boy's chatter. She stops talking.

The room is silent for about three seconds, and the protests begin again. I could join in but don't. The voice's tone sounded a little too familiar. Like my mom's just before she dished out a beating or slap at the least. I back up to one of the empty areas and press against a hard surface. The metal feels wet, but when I check, my hands are dry.

My new friends are focused on that one wall, and before I can think about why the whistle blares again, the even female voice talks, and again, it's shades of my mom the morning after a bender.

I release my pent-up breath when the protests resume. Maybe they understood the words more than I did. Perhaps the message isn't to sit down and shut up as much as it seems to be.

Before I can focus on how this wet not-wet surface is freaking me out, the whistle begins for the third time. The sound is much longer than before, and I have to cover my ears until it stops.

When blessed silence finally returns, everyone looks up at the click from above. A CCTV camera-looking device drops down with a whirr. The lens points at the group of people causing the most of the fuss. They stare back. My vision is getting better with every blink, and the differences among them are striking. Everyone might be buff and tall, but that's the limit of what they have in common. Cat Boy is there, and I think he has a tiger friend. A few have all-black eyes as if they've tattooed the whites out completely. Not only that but they're bald and a little bit gray skinned. Roswell landing wanna-bes, I hope, because anything else is just too weird.

The announcement begins, and now I recognize sounds similar to what's been said before. I have no idea what they mean but have a suspicion. With their attention diverted from the wall, the crowd steps forward to the dropped camera. A few begin yelling and shaking their fists in the air. Others join in.

Laser beams are all I can think to call them as they come out of the camera and mow down the front row of men. Unlike in films, the weapon has no sound. I can't breathe but slide down the wall behind me, in case the thing swivels for the few of us not causing a problem.

I stare while the camera-turned-ray-gun stops moving and slides up into the ceiling. A final announcement is given over the screaming and injured people. My guess is it's saying something like, "You were warned."

The temperature didn't change, but I shiver anyway. The ground doesn't have the false damp like the walls. I focus on touch and don't want to think about what would have happened if I'd continued to pester Cat Boy, now dead, to talk to me.

I know where I am now and am certain Rick wasn't involved. The irrational part of me thinks Cat and his friend Tiger are from one planet. Then the Gray Skin with Tattooed Eyed twins are from another. Not true because space aliens don't exist. Yet, the blood is real. The shooting was real. Normal red blood is pooling under the dead. I take a deep breath and can smell the iron. Plus, I'm pretty sure someone peed when the shots began, and it's a strong odor. Deep holes are gouged out wherever the beams hit. I see someone missing half of his face, and I can't help but shudder.

The saner part of me, the one I'm trying to hold on to, knows this is some sort of crazy mass kidnapping. Because no one looks ordinary, the abductors chose unusual-looking people with muscles. You'd think they'd want wealthy people for the ransom, but okay. No excuse I've invented so far explains why I'm locked up with a bunch of Halloween costumed beefcakes. Overwhelmed and just wanting the headache to stop, I hug my knees and rest my head against them.

Time passes, but I don't know in what increments. After a while, I let go of my legs, and the friends let go of their dead. The lights stay bright, the bodies are left in place, and the sleeping are all awake. Beings who look similar coagulate into groups around the room. Conversations are barely hissed between huddled people who understand each other. I assume it's to avoid another lesson in what quiet time means to whoever is controlling the ray gun. I listen for English or German with no luck.

The people around me look like walking animals. I'm trying to justify why by thinking that's their kink or they're

Halloween fans. Everyone seems like something out of a fairy tale gone wrong. The dog wants to be a man but is stuck halfway. Same with the cat people. Sort of human, but not quite enough. I've noticed how the fishy-looking beings cluster on whatever side of the room is opposite from both furry types. Can't say I blame them if the rest of the universe is anything like Earth and its circle of life.

The similarity of the two-legged creatures in here to our animals leaves me worried. I'm not fond of finding out if there are spider or snake people, or, worse, a rat man. It's real. No prank and this one time? I wish Rick was playing me in all this.

I feel like puking, but where?

Even my cushy butt has its limits, though, and I stand. My legs feel better, but I'm starving and need a toilet. I look around for a door with a sign but nothing. There isn't even a bucket or hole in the floor. Just as I wish for a bathroom, I hear water running. I search for the source, hoping for even a lukewarm drink, only to see someone peeing against the wall. No. Not the type of liquid I was hoping for, not even close.

The sound is making my bladder ache, and I can't blame him for just going. I glance over when the flow stops and am a little surprised at how the shake is universal. And at how his dick matches his greenish gray skin. He reminds me of a toad or maybe a frog. He's built like one, anyway, muscular legs with a beer belly and three chins. Mr. Froggy. A half-crazed laugh breaks out of me, and the guy glares. His huge liquidy eyes narrow and his wide, thin-lipped mouth turns down. I wave a hand as if to say no and pointed to myself. His scowl fades a little before he shrugs and turns away to rejoin his other toad friends. I sigh and slump against the wall. The last thing I need is a bunch of angry amphibians croaking at me.

After stifling another hysterical giggle, I glance over when a metal against metal grinding begins. The part of the room people protested the most is moving as a bin slides out like an ordinary drawer at home. There's a rustle, and from where I can see, pellets fall down. Everyone makes a grab for as many as they can carry. I get to my feet and hurry over as another batch falls to fill the bin. The other stragglers and I also take as many as we can carry.

When I go back to my claimed space, the floor where Mr. Froggy took a leak is gone. As in, there's nothing but a square hole now. The stench is overwhelming as I walk closer, so I back away. I try to not dissect the scents, but death, urine, and feces are unmistakable. The pellets don't seem so appealing even if they're like hardened gummi blocks. I need a new seat away from the sewer and dead bodies.

I'm making my way farther from the cesspool of death while the men crowd around it. When I glance back, they're eating the gummies while peeing. Gag. I find a part of the wet-dry wall to sit against with five or so other women. I still want a restroom but have food and what passes for privacy here.

After a lick and a crunchy bite, the gummi isn't half-bad. It's red but doesn't taste like anything but sweet.

Wherever we are, my guess is our captors want to keep the better behaved of us alive. I'm starving, so I eat without really tasting anything but the oddly tangy sugar. Like the walls, the food is wet but not wet.

I watch to see what people do now their bellies are full, and their housekeeping doesn't disappoint me. Four or five of them drag the several dead men over to the waste trap door and drop them in. I wrap my arms around my knees. A practical part of me thinks they should have frisked the pockets for anything useful for when we're let go. Maybe they know where we're going better than I do.

My bladder is still full, but there's no way I'm squatting in front of everyone. The bin recedes into the wall, and the sewer door slides shut, so I've lost my chance anyway. At least the stench should fade.

A sharp crack, skin against skin, catches my attention. I look along with everyone else, to see a woman struggling out of a man's arms. He's less like Mr. Froggy and a lot more like a Mr. Lizard. His profile is slightly elongated, no lips, solid black eyes. I can see a faint shimmer of scales, and he's a pale green.

The woman he's manhandling, or lizardhandling, is a cousin to the Cat Boys. They're nearby, snickering as she scratches against Mr. Lizard's scales and growling. If all she's managing to do is tickle him with her talons, I'm in serious trouble when they notice me.

The whistle sounds, and I'm the only one who looks up for the false camera. Another voice, male and agitated begins speaking, but the fuss increases. My stomach clenches because I'm pretty sure I know what's going to happen. The camera-type thing slides down and begins firing at the couple. Both fall dead along with several of the bystanders who were cheering him on. People scatter, but the shots stay contained to the small area.

I duck my head, pressing my forehead to my knees in my go-to safe pose. With any luck, the weapon system might keep me unmolested by anyone here. The few females are crying while the men are talking among themselves. I glance up, and the victims' friends are clustered around them.

One of Mr. Froggy's cousins looks at me, pointing, and another of his type taps his arm while shaking his head. I suppose I'm not worth the trouble. For the first time in my life, I'm glad to be considered worthless. That's right, buddy. Hassling me is not worth the trouble.

Wherever we're going, at least this group seems to have learned a lesson.

2

LIN

IF FOOD DROPS AND BATHROOM BREAKS ARE SIGNS OF time passage, we've been in here nine Earth days. How long has it been exactly is a question I'd love to ask anyone in here until I realize my fingernails could tell me. I glance down to see how far my latest manicure has grown. The significant gap tells me I've passed my usual three-week retouch. Not by much, but enough I'd not flash my hands around in public. I ball my fists up more from fear than vanity. I know Rick is probably looking for me. My boss has already fired me. And my mom? I doubt she even knows I'm gone.

Two trap doors open and we're allowed one gummi brick a day, unless their hours are super long. We could be eating three times in one of their days. I have no idea what their measurement of time is. From what I remember about our solar system, Earth and Mars even have different day and year lengths.

What's been nice is how boring the place has been so far. No one is attacking anyone else and getting killed anymore. The protests aren't happening. Even peeing guy waits for the hole in the floor. One of the cat ladies motioned me over a few days ago and guarded while I went. I was terrified of falling in and grateful even if a little leery of befriending a lioness on two feet.

The room, as large as it is, has become hot and stuffy. The smell is worse, too. Nine days of furry or slimy people without water is as foul as anyone can imagine. I both dread and need to escape.

A familiar grinding sounds. Or, I think it's familiar until the pitch deepens. I stand up and look around in case I need to be ready. How the trap door for waste just opened without a sound continues to unnerve me. Some of the passengers with hearing keener than mine stare down at the floor. The smooth metal begins to vibrate underneath, almost tickling the bottoms of my feet until the shaking increases. Those who are standing ease down into sitting. If I didn't know better, I'd swear we were in a plane while the landing gear is being lowered.

The shuddering turns Mr. Froggy's face green, or greener than usual. A few are clinging to each other. I wish I weren't the only Earthling in the group. I close my eyes to keep from throwing up and breathe through the nausea.

Just when I'm convinced the place will bust apart, everything stops. No movement, no noise. Not until a real landing gear sound begins do I open my eyes. Everyone is staring at each other, all of us too stunned to talk. Various sounds come and go, most of them are whirrs or low hums all around us.

The wall I'm backed up against slides up to the ceiling with a whoosh. I scurry away from the influx of cold air.

And...

I don't know where I am except in a clear dome. Mars has two moons, too, right? Only, this place is far spikier and grayer than I've ever seen in Martian images. My smartphone is long gone, or I'd look up other planets in our solar system with two moons. Which is stupid, considering who my co-hostages are. I don't think Mr. Froggy and Ms. Lion are from Venus or Saturn.

A couple of guards appear at the open doorway. They're two mashed-faced men, one wiry, one bulky, and both have gray uniforms. Practical, considering the soil outside. Unlike the canines among us who have a snout of a nose, the guards have Pekinese-flat noses. They wear eye cover, so of course, I'm curious about their iris colors. But not interested enough to flat-out ask, considering the weapons in their hands. I ease back behind everyone else, not wanting to be anything near an example for the others.

The two motion with the tips of their guns and everyone in front of me moves out. I figure staying in the middle would be my best bet in staying hidden. As soon as I'm surrounded, I can't see much except glimpses through the taller people. I scan the crowd and hope there are a few shrimpy people around here, too. Otherwise, I'll be reliving my childhood by needing to climb every countertop just to accomplish basic tasks.

I watch as the door behinds us seals, the air whistles through the uncovered holes, and the forward door opens. The landscape outside is beautiful. Tall, rocky spires lie outside a glittering dome. The two moons, one large with pink splashes of craters, one smaller gray-blue, take up the twilight sky. A setting sun or maybe even suns give the bright clouds a teal color. The same color hugs the horizon and segues into a midnight blue above us. A vast dome overhead goes so far I can't see where it ends on the horizon.

My heart skips a few beats as the realization sets in. Shit. I'm on another planet. Probably light years from home. I'd be in awe and taking millions of photos in nearly any other circumstance. I have no idea how they abducted me or what they want. Hell, I don't even know who *they* are. I stare at everything in case I return home so I can make serious bank on the talk shows. Who cares if they think I'm crazy as long as they pay? I can quit my job and live on the media junket.

They lead us out of the huge airlock, distracting me from my entrepreneurial dreams. I breathe in to get the smell of the place and try to ignore the body odor around me. A cool gust of wind slips through the people around me, and I shiver. My bare toes begin to ache. I cross my arms to try and keep some of my body heat near me. The crowd does help. I'm scared of what happens if we're all separated into pods or whatever aliens do to us here.

A couple more of the flat-faced guards appear and circle us. The extra guards ensure we're herded into a much larger room under the dome. We're all led to a part of the place where walls double the tallest man's height converge until we're forced into a single line. The body heat from those around me fade, and I'm freezing again. I clench my jaw to keep calm as we move forward, step by step. A tall guy with a beagle's coloring in front of me steps into a horizontal and clear tube. I have to follow.

The space is tall enough for anyone here to walk upright yet narrow enough to touch on either side with my elbows. I feel bad for the wider frog men. They had to have been scraping their way down the passage. The enclosed heat is welcome at first. After my chill bumps are gone, the shivering changes to sweating. Still on a mission to make money whenever I'm dumped back on Earth, I smell while staring out of the tube. The air has a damp and metallic quality, and yes, there are two suns.

The beagle guy in front takes a step back, stomping on my bare toes. I stifle a scream and bite into my lip. He looks at me with a grunt before facing forward again. My eyes tear from the pain as I watch a clear vertical tube come down over the lioness in front of him. Her hair is blown or sucked up, and a metal arm comes down to smack her on the neck. As the cover lifts, the floor tilts forward, and she steps off. It's Mr. Beagle's turn. The same isolation, even without the lifted hair, and slap on the neck.

Only with him, I can see some sort of metal disk clinging to his skin. The cover lifts and he steps forward. There's no choice but to step forward, so I do. I look up to see if the place has a hint of lasers because I'm going to scream if it hurts.

The tube comes down, and I thank whoever's listening that I'm not claustrophobic. The vacuum feels rather good, and I relax as my hair is pulled up. If there'd been a shower before the drying, life would be better.

A slap on the neck takes me by surprise. Stupid, I know, but the wormy feeling of my nearby skin crawling afterward bothers me more than the initial hit. Good thing the floor tilts or I'd probably still be standing there with my mouth open. I want to pull the metal off, but the way it's digging into me? Feels like my spine would come out, too.

Not until the stinging subsides do I realize there's a voice talking on this side of the vertical tube. The same one from the cargo ship and even better? I understand what she's saying.

"Single file. Left to dig, right to plant. No exceptions."

People ahead of us are mixing in with others who are covered in the planet's dirt. As the guy behind me is getting his new device, I tap the grimy giant lizard in front of me on the back. "Hello, do you know where we're going?"

He turned his head and hisses, "Shut up, or you'll get us killed."

I don't want to agree, but he's right. Talking might be a crime here. Even with the rebuke, I can't help but grin. This is the first speech I've understood in what feels like weeks. I look up from my navel-gazing and see the right and left doors. A bar of lights over one blinks until someone steps through. Then, the opposite side blinks until the next person. Back and forth as we edge closer to the division. I count back until I discover they'll send me to dig. Which I can't do. I don't have a shovel, and I'm far better at planting, anyway. So plants might die around our apartment thanks to me, sure, but I planted those suckers like a boss. I was born to plant.

Cranky is up and goes right, lucky bastard. I try to sneak in behind him until a metal door slides down, hard. The bottom scrapes my nose and chest, scratching my face. I stumble back, glad I wore my bra to bed for the protection now, and take the hint. Digging could be fun. At least, a lot more fun than being cut in half.

My nose stings, and when I rub it, my hand comes away bloody. Shit. I don't have anything antiseptic and doubt anyone would help if I asked. I lift my shirt's neckline to cover half my face before pressing my nose against the light blue fabric. My best pajamas are ruined, and there's no way to order more.

Shoes.

Shit. I'll need something with a sole if their shovels are anything like Earth's. My toes still ache from Big Guy stomping on them. I suppose I could give him a name like I did Mr. Froggy or Mr. Cat, but really, I can't decide what the hell he looks like. Mr. Lizard and the gang looked like Earth animals. Toe-Cruncher was an ordinary human with a yellowish orange tint. He was dirty enough to have been from what I assume are fields. I refuse to be jealous, even if he's been sent to the outside twice in a row.

And besides, silent bitching about his luck doesn't get me anything to protect my feet. Any sort of shovel will shred my soles. I bite my lip, hoping they give us gear even though I figure they won't. They haven't since this crazy dream began. Why would they now?

After wiping my brow from the now nervous sweat, I listen to see if the announcement has changed. The volume is lower. When I peer around the new guy in front of me, there's a huge gaping hole in the ground. The zigzag of the path into the cave reminds me of Carlsbad Caverns from when I was a kid. Mom was on a sobriety kick and took us there with her boyfriend du jour.

Even though I miss Mom as much as she misses me, I long for my former ignorance of what would happen after the trip. Hell, I should be longing for my former planet, shoes, and whatever coffee I can get. All of us meander down, farther into what I'm pretty sure is a mine. The announcement from up ahead is getting louder as I approach.

"Bust rock. Gently place blue glowing stones on conveyor. Place all cadavers onto conveyor."

"Cadavers? Holy hell," I mutter before putting a hand over my mouth. No one is paying attention, so I let my hand fall. There is a bin of pickax-looking tools rolling up beside a bruiser of a woman several people ahead. She reaches in, and sure enough, it looks like half a pickax. I sigh in relief. My soles are saved.

Before I can blink, she buries the spike into the nearest man. His scream fades to nothing as she pulls the tool free and runs for the entrance. She shoves past me and runs up the switchback path before a familiar whistle blows. "Oh shit." I crouch down just as a buzzing sound grows louder. Flashes of light shine through my closed eyes as the shooting begins. I cover my ears and crouch down when the alien woman and her victims scream.

The buzzing resumes and fades. Feeling the air still, I open my eyes and straighten. Whatever did the killing took out a lot more people than I'd expected. Bodies cover several feet in front of and behind the crazed woman. Another whistle and the announcement resumes. "Bust rock. Gently place blue glowing stones on conveyor. Place all cadavers onto conveyor."

I'm not sure how people are going to comply since the conveyor and other tools are in front of me. And that's okay. I'll just be grabbing my pickax, busting rock, and being nice to any blue glowing stones there to greet me.

The ax is heavier than I thought it would be. The hulks around me made picking up one look easy. I gently put the slightly curved metal end over my shoulder. Easy does it because an aggressive move might trigger the death squad. I follow the man ahead of me.

The mineshaft is damp, like the ones are at home. Cave openings to our left and less often to the right have been chiseled out. The lights strung along a pipe above shine down but not very far into the dark caves. Gates with bars cover every other doorway. Sometimes I can see people inside, but it's dim and no one's moving. I wonder if they're dead but know they can't be. Bodies get tossed on the conveyor like the instructions say.

A trench runs under the gates, and it isn't deep, maybe four inches, and a trickle of water runs down the length. A conveyor moves to our right much like a normal baggage claim belt does at the airport.

I hope the announcement changes soon. Something like, "Bathrooms are to your left. Beds are up ahead. Break time is in five minutes. Steak and lobster for dinner." I never said I was sane.

The motion forward pauses long enough for me to get a longer look into one of the openings to our left. It's still dim in there, but when my eyes adjust, there's just a hollowed-out room. No furniture or lighting.

There are no real landmarks other than support beams every so often. The mine is growing narrower the farther down we go. I've scraped my knee on the conveyor belt's housing a couple of times due to the closeness. The hollowed-out rooms have grown fewer, too. I have no idea how far I've walked until I run into the male in front of me.

"Sorry," I blurt out to the hulk.

He turns to me. "We work here."

"Okay." I turn to tell the guy behind me who's now to my right. "We work here."

Like a giant game of telephone, he tells the next person. I look back at the man to my left, and he's already hacking at the rock over the conveyor. The pieces fall onto the belt as we work. At least our efforts drown out the instructional voice.

I chip away for ages and make a slight dent into the wall. The instructions stopped earlier. I'm not sure when. The blisters on my hands kept distracting me. All of this is bullshit. This isn't what science fiction shows promised at all. I want my hunky starship captain, a food replicator, and warp drive back home.

While I'm daydreaming about some sexy recon team saving me, a blue flash to my left catches my eye. Several of us, including me, stop to stare. A warm azure gem is embedded in the rock. The stone sends out flashes of light. It's beautiful, and I can't help but say, "It must be one of those blue stones the announcer meant."

The amphibian between the new find and me smirks, "You're smart, huh?" before turning back to the loveliness.

Okay, so I'm slow on the uptake. Whatever. "We're supposed to be gentle with them, aren't we?" I manage to squeak out. No one pays attention to me as the one who found the pea-sized stone gives it a hard hit to bust the loveliness free.

A blinding blue light flashes as an explosion shoves me into the worker on my right.

3

TURKH

I'm ready.

The Alliance installed new biologically based nanotechnical systems, or bionans, and reprogrammed me with the latest and greatest system updates. G'nar and I have been given detailed briefs on this planet and the guilty parties using slave labor. We volunteered for this assignment, my first undercover as an Enforcer and his third. While G'nar moved up to Protector in the Intergalactic Alliance's officers program before I did, I've been eager to make up for lost time.

So, we're here to gather evidence with the spiffy new bionans, send it to the Alliance Leaders, and be heroes. Or, at least receive our regular pay and benefits. My first Enforcer assignment seems too easy after the gritty Protector work of rounding up bad guys and transporting them to the Enforcers. Which I now am. My uniform back home has silver edging instead of a rust color. Still gray overall like the Enforcer clothes I wore and much like the Leader uniform I hope to have. The reward of gold edging seems weak, but it's a symbol of the trust the galaxy and empire have in me.

G'nar and I slipped onto the supply ship at its last stop before here. We don't blend in with the Vahdmoshi at all, so we kept hidden near the cargo area. With so many of their systems automated, all we had to do was wait until their sleeping hours before creeping around. Then, once planetside, we blended in with the existing slaves. I scan the area, letting my gaze linger on faces in case the datalinks recognizes anyone in the crowd. No names and details pop up, same as on board the ship.

The Alliance Enforcers first heard about the Vahdmoshi using sixth world abductees a couple of months ago. I don't blame them, except for the freedom regulations. As far as cheap workers go, sixth worlds are the best sources. They're pre-interstellar travel so no one will fight for them. They're humanoid so Alliance tech will work on them. The best part? They're easily replaceable. Sixth world people haven't learned population control. Coupled with their lack of travel, guys like the Vahdmoshi pop in, scoop up a hundred or so at a time, and use them up.

If there's a way to game the system or cheat someone out of damn near anything, the Vahdmoshi will be in the middle of it. They're the jerks of the galaxy. Not the most violent or cruel, no, but certainly the most criminally focused. Most of the time, they're also bad about not thinking through their schemes. I try not to smile at how hard these guys will go down.

They used heat-focused light weapons on board their transport vessel. I noticed them everywhere since they're not difficult to spot if you know what to look for. I also have infrared sight capabilities, which helps. Protectors get them when they sign up for the occupation. Enforcers sometimes need the ability. I suspect the Leaders the next level up the chain of command have grown used to the enhancement.

It's tough to not grin at the future conviction while I record the surrounding humanoids through my optics. There's a line of people in front and a long stretch of them behind me. I recognize all of them as people from fifth and sixth worlds. None of them should be here, never mind being used for a proth mining operation.

I take in each person as much as possible while the two guards herd the crowd into a standard confinement funnel for livestock. Pisses me off to think of how the abducted laborers are treated like animals, but mission comes first. I can wait to be furious later while we're rounding up the criminals.

All of my life, I knew I wanted to serve and protect. I entered the Intergalactic service as soon as they'd take me. A few years patrolling the edge of the Alliance solar systems, a few successes in enforcement, and I was fast-tracked to Enforcer status. Sure, I'm at the lowest level, fact gathering, but still. I am an Enforcer.

Several people ahead of me, an isolation tube lowers,

encircling a female Mrawrn. The movement shakes me out of my thoughts. I do more than record and watch the scene ahead of me. A vacuum pulls her hair up from above so the automatic implant machine can do its work. I wince every time a metal arm smacks the occupant on the back of the neck with a near-obsolete translator. Once it's implanted in me, I'll need to instruct the bionans to modify the programming.

G'nar's thoughts break into my own over our internal communications systems when he asks, *You got a plan to get out of the implant?*

I give him a silent reply by thinking, *Not really.* If I had to be stuck on a low-rent proth mining operation with any other Enforcer, I'm glad he's my partner. He reached this level a few months before I did, staying longer in Protector status than I did. He knows as well as I do we're to blend in, not start a fight the first day planetside. Still, I need to ask him, *Can we tell the bionans to shove out the device if we can't avoid it?*

Hell if I know. They're new to me, too.

I suppress the urge to nod a response since he's a couple hundred bodies behind me in the line. Neither one of us has been undercover for a long time. Forgetting conversational body language might take a minute or two. *Understood.* I notice how the translators glow. Unlike the Mrawrn, neither one of us has hair covering our necks. *We'll have to keep them in place but deactivate or subvert for our own use.*

Agreed.

After a double blink, a systems display superimposes over the scene in front of me. The bionans are a massive improvement over the current nanites with the crisp presentation of my vital signs. The adrenaline spike shown isn't a surprise, so I ignore the warnings. Instead, I send a command to the chip in my brain to auto examine and report on foreign objects as they pierce my skin. Considering my reaction to the new visuals, I also dampen automatic voluntary responses for the next twenty-five hours. Not forever but long enough to get laughing, frowning, or rolling my eyes at what appears to be an imaginary friend whenever G'nar and I talk via the inner communications device.

I observe what sort of humanoids are also in line. There are twenty-three ahead of me by now, and we're all single file waiting for the translator. Every once in a while someone rebels and one of the two guard smacks him in the head. *Interesting how that part isn't automated*, I note before going back to observing. A few burly females stand among a majority of men. The women are Mrawrn with long hair and tails. One of the amphibians from Gleet bumps into a Mrawrn, and her claws extend. Good thing he notices and backs away before she takes a swipe at him.

The guards are Vahdmoshi with flat faces and stubby noses. I've never met a decent one. They talk too loud, take what they want, and are the epitome of brawn over brains. But, since they're the only bipeds armed, I go along with the orders.

Ugly fucker, isn't he?

The bionans have done their job, so I don't snort out a laugh. *So are you,* I retort, *yet I still love you.*

I hear his laugh in my mind even though I'm sure he has his dampeners on as much as I do. G'nar is one of those guys that Leaders hate to promote. He does the work of two people as his standard operating procedure. I thought I had goals down until I met him.

Can you tell what's happening up ahead? After the translators?

I stand up on tiptoe to see over the slightly taller humanoids and answer him with, *A doorway.* I listen, focusing in and beyond the gasps or screams of the newly augmented people ahead of me. *I hear clanging and see shadows.*

Shit.

I know. I try to reassure both of us. He's noticed the hidden and extensive weapons system as much as I have. All of the motion sensors, security bots flying through the air, and automatic light weapons concealed in the ceilings and walls all mean fewer Vahdmoshi guards milling among us to keep the peace. The lack of people in charge around here for us to overpower would mean more instant corporal punishment for slight offenses. I try to be reassuring, focusing my extra hearing and sight farther ahead of us. *No yelling or gunfire,* I send to him.

All right. Be ready for anything.

I don't smile or nod even though the impulses are there. Instead, I transmit, *I might be a little preoccupied in a moment.* There are twelve in front of me, and the process is fast.

Got it. We can talk when we're both done.

G'nar was recruited from a Gharian colony demoted to third world status. I can't help but give him shit sometimes. *If I survive the translator, that is. We advanced races are so delicate.*

Bitch.

Nothing can keep my laugh from being a smile and slight chuckle. Being second world provides a guy with advantages. I like to lord it over G'nar even if we both know we're equals. My amusement fades as the line shortens between me and the automatic implant tube.

Five.

Four.

Three.

Two.

One.

And fuck! I put a hand to the back of my stinging neck. The machine's strength is calibrated way off. If the bionans didn't fix busted blood vessels, I'd have a knot or bruise underneath the electronics. As it is, the translator is moving ever so slightly under my hand.

How'd it go? G'nar asks.

Can't lie, hurts. They need to tone it way down or they'll lose their weaker livestock.

Before I can say it, G'nar does. *That may be their point. Hurts like what?*

The room I'm in now is larger and filled with more

people than those we arrived with. Some humanoids are dirtier than others. *Like a baby's kiss. There's nothing you can do to prepare.*

I'm going to kick your ass.

You can try. The translator they gave me is loose, thanks to the bionans disallowing new hardware without permission. I pull my hand from my neck with the chip in my palm. *I've rejected the implant. Approaching the doorway and there's a divider. Splitting us up as we walk through. No choice.*

Fuck!

I don't laugh at G'nar's pain despite the urge to do so. Before I drop the chip, a thought hits me. *Hold your hand over your neck to hide the removal process and to keep the implant. It probably tracks us.*

Not a problem.

I don't react in front of the guards but follow the new person ahead of me as directed. There's a slight decline and warm air rushes against us. *The smell isn't bad. Like freshly dug dirt mixed with body sweat.*

That's your idea of not bad?

Okay, maybe not so great, either. People ahead of me look back in my direction as if unsure. I figured we'd be hearing from the claustrophobic before now. Adding to my observations, I send G'nar, *the light fades as we descend underground. Looks like I'm in the mines.*

Which way?

I also glance back to see him at the doorway before I drop a little farther and lose sight. *Left.*

30

There's a pause before he thinks to me, *Shit. I'm going right. The air is already cooler, and I can see outside through an opening as big as a starcraft hangar door.*

G'nar is going to be as cold as I will be hot, I figure. Every few steps seem to increase the air temperature, and I begin sweating.

This silence is unusual but not a surprise, so I ask, *Status check?*

Ow! Fuck! Fuckers need to recalibrate.

Yeah, he's reached the translator assignment tube. I tell him, *Remember to keep your implant intact but deactivated.*

Hurts like a...okay. I'm good. Going to the right, outside. Looks like there's tall...spiky mountains and...trees...

I frown when his transmission is reduced to every few words. *I'm losing you,* I think at him, trying to interrupt his report.

Can't ping the Alli...main data off...

I try a few more times to reach him but nothing. After a few attempts, I can't hit the Alliance main datalinks, either. I'm worried but not panicked. We have protocols for any type of separation. In fact, our leaders want us to split up if possible. Two different sets of information will help the case exponentially.

Still, I don't like being cut off from my only backup like this. We were just supposed to get in, record evidence, and get out. No heroics and no arrests. Especially not when our supreme director wanted the entire government taken down and not just the peripheral bad guys.

I press the crude translator to the back of my neck, wincing as the spikes break the skin. After a quick update to the bionans, the translator winds the nerve uplinks through my spine. The majority of the device's systems are turned off in favor of my superior ones. I have my programming leave the tracking and integration algorithms intact. We'll need to hijack their internal communications with our own when we're ready. I'm looking forward to wiping the planet's information.

Without chatting with G'nar to distract my biological mind, I can look around at the people and the environment. The mine we're all descending into has switchbacks down the shaft. Along with hot air, voices float up. I can't help but grin at fourth world people's enthusiasm when realizing their translators work. It's somewhat adorable. The deeper we go, the louder, hotter, and less supervised we seem to be.

No guards? I don't buy it. What's waiting for us at the end of this tunnel?

No way this many different people are tossed underground to work without adult supervision. I want to hit up G'nar, see if he's noticed, but unless I'm on the surface at the same time he is, not gonna happen.

The shuffling line stops dead in front of me. I mumble a, "sorry," to the humanoid in front of me when I stumble into him. Mumbani, I think. He's staring into the mine, so I do, too. A scuffle has broken out between two people, and I can't help but watch. A much larger male is pawing at and slapping a smaller humanoid. She seems female even if I can only see her light-colored hair and a little of her body. They shift and I get a better look at the two. I don't know how the hell *she* came here. She's too small and barely dressed for the work our director suspects is going on here. They need to calm down because if the enforcement systems the Vahdmoshi have in place works, all of us are targets.

A low hum zips past my shoulder, and I duck, never taking my eyes off of the two. The security bot hovers above them. I don't want to watch but need to for evidence. The bot shoots at the couple and around them. He falls over on top of her. From what I can tell, she and several other innocents are dead, too.

The bot lifts a few feet, shoots again, hits a couple more people, and leaves. I don't breathe or shut off my recording until the hum fades. The line begins moving, slower and jammed where I know at least seven bodies lie.

It takes a good ten minutes before I pass by the corpses. Only five, which is odd, and now I'm curious. As we walk farther into the mine, natural light gives way to dimmer artificial lighting. I increase the infrared and scan where I think the female would be by now. If she's from Earth, to hell with the illegal mining. The Vahdmoshi are going down for primitive contact violations.

While I'm looking for her, I examine the other workers. They aren't essential to catalog because we're after the offenders. Considering the detainees' lack of tech, it's a miracle any of them survived the trip here. Despite the emotional movement dampeners, I shake my head with a sigh. This is far bigger than our orders hinted. The addition of primitive races will impact Alliance leadership up to the Emperor at a time when the stability is already threatened by an assassination attempt.

It's been a long time since I've been this worried.

The path has widened enough for us to walk two or three across. An intense line of heat on someone up ahead catches my eye. The person, I think it's the female who fought with the dead guy, turns to look behind her.

Holy pless of Tunsa. It's an Earther. I mean, she's an Earther. Part of me wants to hurry and catch up to her. She's a sixth world person and rare. Her race is infinitely collectible to more advanced species, and I wonder why they'd dump her here. Earthers' various appearances make them valuable on the black market. They're one of the youngest races of humanoids in the galaxy and are already reaching for the stars. Only seventh worlders are newer and less developed. While I enjoy learning about the seventh world civilizations, I find speech-evolved Earthers and their planet infinitely more interesting.

I thought the Vahdmoshi were doomed with their kidnappings at the fifth world level. Now I know they're fucked. Even without the illegal mining charges, stealing her means the Alliance members of the Vahdmoshi are finished. The Charter is precise on the few statues listed. The document drawn up by all of the members is forgiving due to the different cultures in the galaxy. "No contact with less advanced worlds" is second on the list after "do no harm to another." The last time a system didn't take the law seriously was the last time anyone heard from them. They may still exist, and if they do? The Intergalactic Alliance has no knowledge of their fate after the ruling, having wiped our datalinks clean of their presence.

With the Earther here, my job of gathering evidence and getting back to my homeworld is even more critical now.

4

LIN

My upper arm is killing me, but I can't take the time to cry. The pain flows in a line straight to my neck. I glance at the wound for the first time. There's a burn mark cutting across my pajama sleeve and down into my arm. Damn. It's not bleeding, so I do what I can to ignore it. The crowd of humanoids flows around the assailant and me. I climb to my feet, fall in line, and try to ignore the deep stabbing burn as I go. Like last week, month, whenever my first time here was, I grab a pickax.

My second time deep underground in a sweltering mineshaft fills me with dread. I look up the switchback path and to the cavern's opening. One last gathering of natural sunlight before there is none.

An exceptionally tall male stands between me and the sun. The light is too bright for me to see him. Reminds me of looking into an oncoming car's headlights. I miss driving, fast food, and television so much. The man's shape would get him laid back home, but with the movement downward, I'm pushed to face forward and follow along.

I've learned a lot more about the mining system since I arrived. The mineshaft goes deeper at an angle steep enough for water to flow downhill. Every so often, there's a tunnel to our right where the shaft used to end before making a turn up toward the surface. The conveyor belt went through the tunnels, too, and carries food to us while taking bodies and blue stones back to the surface. Caves were dug out to our left. We sleep there, or try to, anyway. People have nightmares, snore, hassle each other. Exhaustion helps in getting and staying asleep.

We pass the point where I spent the last time down here. Not that it was so long ago. They ordered us up to the surface to mingle with everyone else. Fun, if you like pushy crowds and being grabbed at by males of all species.

So no, not fun at all.

The line slows and stops quite a ways farther down. I turn to the wall and hit the rock using both arms. My left vibrates with the blow, and I cry out from the pain. I let my arm hang limply while hacking at the rock in front of me. The pick misses a couple of times and the point arcs down towards my legs.

After the third time of a near miss, I let the ax fall and rest the handle against my thigh. The flyaway hair clings to my face thanks to the hot damp down here. I brush it away and glance to my right to see how close the Greek god ended up being from me.

He's one man over and staring right back at me. His

eyes are black pools of obsidian to go with his honest-to-God metallic skin. If I didn't know better, I'd say someone spray painted him with bronze. The practical side of me knows it's sweat coating him, but still. He's fine.

I give a smile in greeting, and he scowls before turning back to his own section of the wall. Not friendly, huh? I pick up my handle and resume what busting I can. There are sensors in the ground. Or at least I think so based on what's happened when people took too long of a break during work hours.

Even cranky, the god's face is beyond handsome. He'd be on every magazine's cover back home. The slight scruff of facial hair would leave them swooning on social media. I sneak a peek again. He makes busting the semi-soft stone around here look like breaking up dry bread.

Which makes me hungry and I don't want to think about food. Yummy, perfect-in-every-way Earth food. Heck, I'd even eat beef liver at this point. Anything but the literal slop they feed us here.

I'm lost in how perfect fast food was until Mr. God breaks up my trance with a wave and a nod toward the wall in front of me. I roll my eyes before resuming the work. It's nice he cares, though. After a solid tap, the cakey stuff falls away, and a tiny bit of a blue stone glows. My first, as small as a grain of rice, and it's beautiful. Everyone stops digging around me, and we all stare. I need to remove some of the rock around the gem so it'll fall onto the conveyor belt.

As soon as I lift my ax, someone bellows to my right.

"Don't! You'll kill us all!"

Mr. God pushes aside the two men between us and jerks away my ax. The pull jostles my whole body and my injured arm stings. I yell at him, angry from the pain. "Son of a bitch! Warn a girl next time, would ya?"

He throws the ax onto the ground and edges to the gem. "You have no idea what metal does to proth, do you?"

"Uh, yeah. How do you think I got all of these scars?" I point to my left side from last month's burn. "The guy who hit the last gem died next to me."

He glances up before going back to tenderly digging out the stone with his fingers. "Scars? You're lucky you look so good. Hitting this will leave nothing of you."

"Oh?" I like how he thinks I look good. There are zero reflections around here, and Mr. Gorgeous God is obviously very smart. "I can't tell. I've spent the past month, if they have months here, hoping I'm not disfigured."

He glances up for a moment and examines my face. "There's some healing left to do, but you're not too scarred."

Hmm, no "let me take you in my arms, you gorgeous woman"? Shit. "Good, okay." A familiar buzzing begins, and I look towards the tunnel opening. "Look, you'd better get back to work. They know we're slacking." No one says anything. I turn back to the crowd, and the god has uncovered a blue gem as big as a baseball from the dirt.

His hands are really something. Big, strong, sexy. If he actually smiled at me once, I'd bet his strong and sturdy fingers could play me like anything otherworldly. He gently coaxes the gem from the hard but spongy ground as if tickling a baby. "Wait, that's how big it was?"

"Yes. Your next strike would have been your last." He pauses to breathe for a few seconds before going back to the stone.

I don't want to admit it, but he's right. The entire mine could have caved in over my scattered body. "I promise to be a hell of a lot more careful."

"You have no idea how dangerous this is," he growls before wiping his forehead with the back of his hand. "Work in my place. There's no more for you to find and we can switch back when I'm done." He glances up for a second. "Go, now."

"Fine." I take my ax and begin working in his spot. Wonder how he knew his place has no gems for me to kill us with? I glance at him between hits. If there weren't already several men here vying for the term Mr. CrankyPants, I'd give him that name. Giving a few blows hard enough to keep the enforcements away, I sneak peeks as he works.

The work I'm doing now is so lax because I'm just watching his arms flex with tension as he more than gently places the gem on the belt. I sigh when he stands, his height perfect for his proportions. I'd read somewhere about how thinking of sex decreases pain. He's the first man here who could take away a lot of aches for me.

When he comes over to me in his former area, I step

back. "Thank you, Mr. God—um, mister. I appreciate your help and owe you one."

One of the hairy-faced guys between us gurgles a laugh. "If that's all it takes to get your ass, baby, let me dig your stone next time."

"What? No. That's not what I meant."

"Too bad." The fox guy doesn't stop his steady bash of the wall opposite us. "Owe me a fuck, and I'd make you see the stars and cry out for your momma."

Men like the fox guy are why I sleep out in the main tunnel when I can. It's horrible and exhausting, but anything to avoid rape. He tilts his head toward the hole in the wall behind us. "How about next rest period, you let me take my thanks in advance?"

"Really think she's worth it?" Mr. God says. "I don't."

I roll my eyes at the bronze guy as he takes off his shirt and I go back to my spot. "Good. You're not worth a lot, yourself." Not that he cares, given what the man looks like half dressed.

After a peek at the bare-chested Mr. God, who might have had a chance before his previous comment on my worth, I frown. Not even if he were the last fur-free humanoid on whatever rock this is. Not happening, either.

The two men chat, and I try to ignore them. Smashing rock drowns them out a little but not enough. I hear the deep and lust-stirring voice of Mr. God.

"You like being watched, huh? Everyone has their kink, but as for me? I don't think poking her is worth dying for."

My ax pauses as I realize he means me. Before I can even think about how pissed I am, Fox replies to him.

"Just wait. You been here as long as I have, you'll start looking at those food packs with a hungry dick."

"Oh gag," I mutter as the two stay focused on what soft foods are the best to screw. I just want to drown them out with my pickax. At least the disinterested Mr. God is a safe guy to sleep with, as in, actually sleep with tonight. Or day. I have no idea how long the sunlight lasts on this planet. Yet another reason to weasel my way into the planting area instead of this sauna hell.

The new best friends ever seem to have run out of shit to talk about if going by their silence is anything. I sigh and wipe the ever-present sweat from my brow. My stomach is growling, and I wish they'd send the food bin downstream to us. The conveyor belt runs slower during dinnertime.

Hack, hack, hack, until finally, the belt slows. Everyone cheers without stopping the work. I can tell who the new guys are due to their lost expressions. At least, I think that's what a new frog guy's face looks like. Their eyes are always too big for their faces.

The bin full of food packs makes its way to us. I can't see any at the angle I'm in, so I know a lot has been taken. I have to hurry and reach way inside to grab one for myself.

"Break time is 20 sectars."

I'd love it if the time were longer. As I take my seat between the bronze guy and his new friend, not giving them a chance to drag me into a room alone is fine, too.

"So this is my new lover, huh?" Mr. God squeezes the bag and sniffs. "What is it?"

Fox speaks before I can. "Whatever they've grown up top. We plant and pick leaves for the mush before it's served to us."

"Huh." He takes a bite or sip and makes a face. I can't help but laugh because I did the same thing my first time. He glances at me with a grin. "Tastes like something a pajii shits."

I have no idea what a pajii is but suspect it eats grass without chewing. I also don't say anything but finish my meal. His earlier remark still rankles my ego.

"Hey, Earther, ever have anything like this at home?"

He gives me a shit-eating grin, and it's gorgeous. I'm a little thrilled he's paying attention to me, but still, I want him to work for me. I give him my best raised eyebrow stare. "You talking to me?" I say, although no one has a clue about the movie reference. Or what a movie even is.

He glances around as if really searching for someone. "I don't see any other Earther here, so I must be."

I ignore what his smile does to my insides and snort a laugh, wishing these guys knew the context. "Yeah, only it's a lot like something a cow would shit."

Mr. God sits up and leans forward. "Herbivore with several stomachs? Raised for its meat?"

This guy has been around the galaxy, and I grin. "That's the one."

"Wait." Fox blocks us. "Earthers raise animals for food?"

His revulsion is a bit puzzling. Foxes at home ate small animals, I thought. Or did they? Maybe not with the way this guy has his snout wrinkled. "What, you all don't?"

"No." He shudders. "No. We're an advanced species."

"A lot of Earthers eat meat." I shrug and resist the joys of describing my last medium rare steak. "Doesn't mean we're not advanced." I did, after all, go to college.

Before he can reply, the announcement begins. "Resume work. Bust rock. Gently place blue glowing stones on conveyor. Place all cadavers onto conveyor."

I get to my feet. "This song is so old."

"What do we do with these?" Greek god asks while holding up his empty food pack.

"Drop them," I answer, and one of his eyebrows rise. "I know. I had trouble leaving my trash behind the first few times. A worker comes along and picks them up." After checking up the shaft, I nod to our right. "There he is now."

"What does he do with them?"

"I don't know. Recycle, dump in a pit, refill and give to us again?" He trades places with Fox which is a bit surprising. He's next to me now and reminding me silently of how tall he is. I manage to squeak out, "I've not been here long enough to know anything."

"Me either." He watches as the cleanup crew of one walks up to, behind us, and beyond. "They should automate his work, too."

I begin working again. "Automate all of this so I can go home."

"To somewhere you call Earth?"

I nod and grumble, "That's the one, and I'm almost afraid you know the name."

A silence stretches out before he says, "You'll never see your home again."

My pick falters, and I hit the belt with the tip. He's an asshole who has to be kidding me. He's also wrong. He has to be. "Yes, I will. I will go home when whatever this is, is over."

He pauses before resuming with a determined clench to his jaw. "No. You need to accept it's not ever going to happen. No one will allow you to return to Earth."

[5]

TURKH

WELL, THAT WENT BETTER THAN I THOUGHT IT would. She's laughing at our law about traveling to Earth. I figured screaming, crying, coming at me with the pick, and then denial. She went straight for disbelief.

Up close, her hair is this rare gold I've never seen in real life before. I keep trying to figure out her eye color, too, but she's always in motion. She has a stubborn expression on her face as she hits the rock and says, "Whatever. You know nothing."

I laugh. I might not know anything, but my database holds a galaxy of information. "Really?"

The woman grimaces as the pick skips across the harder rock and she sighs. "Yeah, nothing, or you'd be flying around in a starship instead of being down here with me."

She has a point, and I do miss my craft. Saying anything about the law like I know how the higher worlds

47

live was a rookie mistake. If I'm lucky, she'll forget what I've said. Her disbelief is good, though. I can use it to my own advantage. "You're right. Anyone else would be flying away by now."

I glance over when her work rhythm becomes erratic. She continues to wince every time her pick hits the rock. I know she has to be in pain from the earlier wounding. "Am I the only person you've talked to down here?"

"Not hardly. I've talked to others."

She's quiet for a while, and the suspense gets to me. I have to push for more. "And?" I glance at her when her movement stops. "What did you learn?"

"They don't know anything, either." She begins busting rock again. "Some have been up on the surface in the fields and talked about what it's like up there. They've said it's a lot colder. I almost want the cool after being down here for a while."

G'nar and I knew going in what the climate here would be like. I'd expected the mines to be the same as the surface, but it's warmer than even body heat and mechanics can explain. With her thin little shirt, short pants, and bare feet, the woman would freeze in the fields. "Be glad you're down here. You're not dressed for anything colder."

"No shit, Sherlock. They grabbed me while I was sleeping in my pajamas." She shakes her head before giving me a grin. "I don't suppose you know who Sherlock is?"

Having zero access to my central database means my Earth knowledge has a serious limit. "Not at all."

"Never mind." She stops for a second to look at me with eyes matching the color of her blue clothes. "Except, don't you watch Earth television to learn our ways? That's what all the smart aliens do."

"Pless no." Most sixth world broadcasts were required viewing in Xeno history classes. I've had enough to last me for a very long time. "There are faster and easier ways to learn anything than watching your television. Smart natives learn which ignorant aliens to ignore."

I try to not laugh when she frowns at me. Her irritation is cute. She's so fair, more so than some of the people on my homeworld. I grin as it occurs to me in a flash how what I know of her planet is not what we're supposed to be talking about at all. I'm down here as an undercover backward slave. Not the best time to be chatting up a pretty woman. "Our civilization only had what was on our planet, anyway."

"How did your kind know about Earth?"

Considering how she's favoring her left arm, I feel like I've teased her enough for one day. There's no need for me to tell her my favorite "how many Earthers does it take to pour water from a shoe" joke. Particularly since she's not wearing any. Too low of a blow at the moment. I clear my throat and say, "Rumor. We had contact with an advanced race, and they mentioned you."

"Oh great. I'm not sure I want us to be so well known considering where they've put me."

"Too late. Nearly everyone in the galaxy knows about your planet. It's actually one of the most hospitable ones for life. A vacation spot." And, I'm talking too much again. Shit. It's like she's like one of my nephews and I want to show her everything interesting.

I'm on a mission, not on a play date, so I add, "The others here know more about Earth than I do and I've heard a few things." When I glance at her, she's looking at me, the fear in her eyes easy to read. I want to reassure her but don't know how to without making everything worse. Maybe hint at the Alliance and the fact her world is restricted from all visitations? It's worth a try. "All this is supposed to be against the law."

She stops and turns toward me. "What law? Is there a governing body for the universe or even this part of the galaxy? Do you know who I can report a kidnapping to around here?"

All right, so I'm digging in deeper. I can't say anything else and need to turn this conversation around, quick. "I don't know. I don't even know who's in charge around here."

"I see."

After a while, I realize she's done talking. A shame, because I liked hearing her voice. I can restart the conversation with her later. Right now, I need to organize all of the input from the time we landed until now. The repetitious work gives me a chance to zone out and catalog information stored in my systems. Hopefully, G'nar is able to transmit as he records. Otherwise, I'll just need to absorb as much as possible before finding a break in the interference.

The report doesn't take long, a few milliseconds and I'm ready for the next chance to transmit. Might as well make small talk with the Earther. Our mission director added sixth world information to the Alliance datalinks at the last minute, so I know a little about the woman's planet. This is my only chance to talk with a real Earther and I can't resist saying, "I'm Turkh, by the way."

"Just Turk?"

She doesn't make the soft "h." It shouldn't matter, no, but it does, so I repeat the sounds. "Turk-h."

She laughs and leans over towards me. "Ohhh, it's like that, Turk-ha?"

Pless. She sounds a lot like my cohorts at the primary school. "No. No ha to it."

"Sorry," she says but doesn't look as if she's apologetic. "I'm Lindsey Daniels, but everyone calls me Lin for short."

"Ah. My full name is KirKrellTurkh." Unlike everyone on Ghar, Earthers have naming traditions all over the place. Named after fathers, mothers, places, anything goes. "Your translator knows enough and doesn't give you the meaning. My father, Kir, had a son, or a Krell, and named me Turkh."

"That's rather poetic, and you're right. I would have called you Kirk or just Turk."

I clench my teeth and smile. Yeah, and manage to ignore the need to add the "h" to her pronunciation. "I wouldn't have answered to my father's name."

"No, and I rarely answer to Daniels." She stops for a moment to rest. "My arm hurts like a bitch right now."

I've kept my eyes open for a medkit since entering the mineshaft but found nothing. "Here, let me have your tool for a moment."

She snickers a little before handing it over. "I might need your tool later for the pounding."

Odd thing to say, but all right. I shrug. "Take it to do what you want after you rest for a while." I use my right arm to hit my area and the left to hit hers. "Any time you need my tool, just ask." She snorts again before growing silent. I glance over to see her angling her injury to one of the lights overhead for a better look.

Processing the odds of breaking the law by how much I can tell her, I decide to give a little information to reassure her. "Did you taste the bitter in our meal today? The hint of..." She doesn't have schril on Earth, and I don't know her words for what compares to the medicine.

"Like ground up aspirin?"

"A pain reliever?" At her nod, I return her grin. "Yes, it's a pain reliever. I can tell they've added it and probably a few other compounds to our food."

"Jesus, like what? Do you have super taste buds, or does your world have this sort of technology? And if you do have tech able to modify your senses, how do you not have a way out of a hell hole like this?"

There's so much to break down in her monologue, and I don't know where to start. Keeping the mission safe at the top of my mind, I begin with the easy explanations. If nanotechnology gives me a super taste ability I can explain away as organic, I'll go with it. "Yes. We're all able to pick out specific flavors where I'm from. Very common." It's true, too. By the time we're ten sas old, we're given basic nanos.

"Do you have the ability to travel between planets or solar systems?" She reaches for her tool and I debate for a millisecond before giving it back. "You seem more intelligent than most of the others here."

I won't lie, her considering me better than those around us gives my ego a huge boost. I also lean closer to her so the Blendarian on her left side won't hear. "You're biased because our appearance is similar. Our ancestors followed a similar path and give us a common bond."

Lin, now that I know her name, resumes her mining. "If I weren't getting tired and the medicine you discovered in our food wasn't wearing off, I'd make you tell me more about your history."

I ignore her backhanded request and watch her work. She's still using just one arm. The urge to take over for her is strong. Lin's smaller than I am. No surprise. Most Earthers are. There's a calmness about her that I find concerning, though. "How long have you been here?"

"No idea. I couldn't even begin to guess." She looks down at her fingernails. "My nail polish says two months."

I peer down to see if she has a display but see nothing but dark pink and chipped paint has grown out from the base. "How? I don't see anything there other than color." We'd have information on our fingerpads since the skin is thinner there, but even if the nails could display something, no one I know would cover the readout.

She smiles. "You don't have polish, huh? I have an idea of how long it takes for my manicure to grow out. I'd say two months, but that's on Earth and assuming the goo is as nutritious as my usual diet." Her next stroke misses the rock and hits the belt. "The workdays feel like forever."

Her injury is on the other side of me. "Here, let me have your tool again. I want to see your arm." I put down my implement and reach for hers.

Lin does as I've requested and I begin doing her work and mine. After she looks up and down the corridor, she says, "You're spoiling me."

"It won't be for long. Turn and let me..." As she does, I see what's happened much more clearly. The shot cut her sleeve in two and scraped a canyon into her arm. My own aches in sympathy. "I'm sorry I can't do anything to help."

"Don't be, it's fine."

The Blendarian stops working and says behind me, "Let me help you sometime, sweetheart. Sometime when we're supposed to be asleep, and I'll work for you all night long."

"Thank you, but no. No one needs to be working for me at all." She tries to take her tool back, and I resist. "Come on, Turkh. I don't want to owe anyone favors." She nods at the Blendarian before leaning closer to add, "You understand?"

"I guess I do." She gives another tug, so I let go. "Sorry. I just don't enjoy watching someone suffer."

She hits at the rock again. "Suffer is a strong word, but my arm does ache all the way to my neck and teeth. But, it could always be worse. I consider how my body could be rolling along on the belt to God knows where right now, and suck it up."

The idiom "suck it up" has no entry in my memory, so I store the phrase for later. I give another strong ping to G'nar and the outside world, but nothing. Pless it. Hundreds of solutions run through my processors, and none can be implemented due to the Lesser Worlds order. I absolutely cannot give her a single one of my nanos to repair the damage.

We're silent for a while. Others talk to each side of us. I've been half listening to the Blendarian and Gleetar talk about sexual differences in their women. Cross female Gleetars off of any list, I tell my main goal list. Especially if they look similar to the males with big bellies, wide mouths, huge eyes, and are perpetually damp. I'm not a speciesist by any means but like my women to have drier skin.

Lin pauses to wipe sweat from her forehead. "I think I've talked to you more today than I have anyone else since I've been here."

She's rather lovely, and I smile at her for a moment. As she pulls the hair away from her face, I respond with, "I'll take that as a compliment."

"Or as a future career option. You'd make a great counselor."

The word comes back with several meanings from her

planet. I'm already an Enforcer for the Alliance, similar to but not equal with her councilor. "A what?"

"Right, someone who listens to your problems and helps solve them."

I nod at the explanation. "Listening is my job."

"Other than finding gems, huh?" As a tone sounds, Lin stops working to touch the back of her neck. "Oh thank God. I'm so ready to stop." She lets her tool fall to the ground. "Shift change." The gates behind us move. "I didn't think I was going to live through this one." Metal grinds against the porous rock as several of the dug-in doorways are unblocked. She glances up at me. "Leave your ax here and hurry."

"What?"

"Stop gawking, seriously. It's time to quit, and we have to go." She grabs my hand and pulls me toward one of the newly unbarred openings. "Isn't your neck buzzing right now?"

I'd forgotten about the primitive translator my nanos rejected until she mentioned hers. My instructions turned off everything in the alien tech except the homing device. Up the mineshaft, a blast of water goes off multiple times before groans and curses echo down to us. I look at Lin and she explains, "The others are getting cleaned up to work. The opening in the bars will shift to let them out."

I watch the base of the exposed cavern as a small river of sewage flows down the narrow trench. Hideous smell, too. Lin pulls me farther down the mine with her. "We need to find somewhere not so stuffed full of people." She and I duck inside a damp and dark room. Between the cleaning, outside sewer, and press of fresh-off-the-shift miners, the air stinks. The Blendarian follows us inside while the Gleetar watches the gates move to shut us in. When the metal stops grinding, damp people start milling past our opening while on their way to a place along the rock wall. Right in front of me, someone, a silver-skinned MoNse with large, black, and slanted eyes picks up a discarded ax to begin his work. Water still drips off of him.

The events make me wonder what G'nar is dealing with on the surface. Being holed up in a shallow cave makes my hair stand on end. I don't fear small spaces, but the room is more like a wide tunnel, double the size of the mine shaft. The dim room won't let me see much, so I switch to infrared. Now that I can't see her very well, I miss being able to watch her colors shift hues in various lights. No one from my world has color in her eyes like she does. I'll bet she can't see a hand in front of her face or anyone coming up to attack her. "Are you sure this is where we need to be right now?"

"Yes. Be glad you're here." She settles in against a wall and slides down to sit. "It took me one time of missing the chance to sleep before I learned to hustle." She pats the ground next to her, and I sit, too. "When you're out there, you're expected to work without stopping for anything but bathroom and food breaks. I can't find the cameras watching us, but they know when we're not hitting the rock."

My concern for her, their, treatment overrides

everything else. "Did you learn this punishment first hand?"

"Yeah, a couple of times." She closes her eyes and leans back to rest her head against the rock. "I was stupid the first time. Thought I could just quit and walk away since no one was watching." She sighed. "Those translators can be such a bitch when you slack off too long."

Her using the word "first" piques my curiosity. Plus, I need to get this down as evidence. "Was there more than once?"

"Afraid so. The second wasn't my fault. You've seen what happens when a fight breaks out. Everyone involved tends to die. Some almost normal-looking guy wanted to play with me instead of work. After that, no one messed with me until today."

Pless, her normal probably meant another Earther down here. "Almost normal-looking to you?"

"As much as a hairless blob of a man can be." She settles in against the rock. "He'd have been somewhat odd with the whites of his eyes tattooed black, but back home a few people have had the same thing done. His pale skin and bald head are somewhat more common."

Interesting that a MoNse could blend in on Earth. No wonder she'd kept a good distance from the one near us earlier. I make a note to the currently running recording to check for Vahdmoshi infiltration on that planet. "Was today the third time you'd been accosted?"

"Yeah. Surprised me, too. He must have been a new guy." She opens her eyes and stares across the room at

LIN'S CHALLENGE

the Blendarian and a Mrwarn finding their places to sleep. "I don't expect it to last much longer. Workers are going to get in better shape. They won't be as exhausted, and I hope I'm able to keep up with them physically, too."

One of the Gleetars who made it in before the doors closed wanders over to the doorway. He begins to relieve himself, and I'm glad the room slants down to the trench outside.

"In case you couldn't guess, that's the restroom. Mr. Frog and his crew know to go there. Mr. Fox and his buddies still want to pee against the wall. I haven't seen a dolphin since we landed, so I assume they're all upstairs."

I understand some of her words but not all and have to ask what she means. "Restroom, fox, frog, and dolphin?"

"Sorry. Elimination area? Shitter? What do your people call where you go...you know?"

I have to laugh because "shitter" translated just fine. "Waste room, usually. We have a bath room for bathing only."

"Makes sense. The other words I used are names for various animals on Earth. Different people remind me of certain animals at home." She yawns. "I never expected aliens to look so familiar and yet so strange at the same time."

A true statement if I ever heard one. "Me too." I lean over to find a more comfortable spot next to her against the rock wall. I try to tell myself about the worse situations I've been in, about how much rougher I had it while working as

59

a Protector. Doesn't work. The wall is still bumpy as a backrest.

I'd love nothing more than a cool shower and my bed. I take my shirt from my pants pocket and put it on. The fabric smells as bad as I'd expect and I grin at how soft I'm getting. I've only been an Alliance Enforcer for a couple of sas. Suspecting the answer isn't one I want to hear, I ask, "Where do we wash up? The system cleans the room, but does it clean us, too?"

"Yes, in here. It's dark so you can't see it now, but you remember how the above pipe runs into the room?"

I glance up and find the dark line of a cold bar attached to the warmer-hued ceiling. "I do."

"Those points aren't gun barrels like I'd thought at first. They're spray nozzles. We're given a cold shower before we're let out to work. Chilly, but somewhat gentle."

I nod. "They must bring it in from outside instead of underground. It's probably part of the irrigation system for the terraforming happening under the dome above us."

"This is my first day in this area. I don't know if it's warmer this far below the surface. Anyway, the water after the bars open is much worse. If you're not out of here quick enough, you're sprayed like the rest of the room. I'd say it resembles a fire hose if you had any idea what I meant." She fidgets again, bumping into my arm. "Sorry. It's dark."

"You're fine," I reassure her, which is adorable. She's obviously tough to have survived a month down here, yet, she's delicate, too. Her hitting me had zero effect. "You'd have to work harder to hurt me." I can't help but smile when she laughs before leaning against my arm as if I'm a huge pillow.

"If it weren't for the security around here, I'd accept your challenge before giving up in defeat." Lin presses the side of her face against my bicep, and I smile. My system works to keep my temperature lowered down here. It's clear she's enjoying the coolness and says, "If I weren't so tired, I'd ask you all about what's going on. Have you fill in all of the blanks I don't know."

I've been careless. She suspects I know far more than I'm supposed to. She might be easy to talk to, but I'm the one to blame for being so open with her. In an effort to dial the information back a notch or five, I say, "You could probably tell me, instead. I've been here an entire day and still don't know when our holidays will be." She chuckles against me, and I can't help but smile. "I'm serious. You know the sanitation, security, and housing systems far better than I do."

She puts a hand on my forearm. "Ah, but you knew about the blue gems and where they were better than I did today. I might have killed us all without your insight."

Since I can't tell her my advanced optics lets me pick out aberrant energy patterns, I go with, "The gems just speak to me."

"Oddly enough, I understand. One of my friends can find four-leaf clovers like a boss." She pauses before explaining, "Three leaves are the usual and four abnormal.

She says the unusual ones seem to glow. Probably like the gems do for you."

I turn my head toward her and breathe in before replying but stop as a rush of pheromones flood my lungs and senses. The allure of her grips me harder than a charkin's chain. All I want to do is remain still and inhale her scent in until every molecule of my air is hers. I close my eyes as the smell shoves out every other thought. The system display in my mind reads, "98% genetic match. Begin union?"

Pless. Pless it all. The Earther has awakened me. This can't happen. Not now, not with her, ever.

Everything, including this notification, is recorded for the director. I can't erase anything. At best, I can mark it as private. She's still against me, only now I can feel her touch on a cellular level. No wonder other Gharians seem to be so singularly focused on their union partner. I haven't even accepted the match, and I want more of her.

Accept match?

Now it's a voice in my head. I want to refuse, but the need to accept overwhelms me. How did we stay in control before nanotech? *Pause match*, I think in reply.

I should delete. She can't be sent back home, yet I doubt we'll be able to unite and live together.

Accept and unite?

I groan out loud, and Lin looks up at me. "Am I too heavy?" She begins to move away. "I'm sorry, but you're so cool and refreshing."

Delay union, I reply to my system before smiling at

Lin. "I don't mind at all. You're a little bit of fluff, and I'm able to keep both of us comfortable."

She laughs and settles in again. "A perfect match."

Union delayed. Match accepted.

I smile at how bad I thought things were a moment ago. Now they're infinitely worse. Lin has accepted for both of us. I could override my system but not my base instinct.

Usually, when we're at the mercy of mating biology, it's with a legal person. I glance down at her and mentally relax my body. The push-pull of wanting to complete our union with sex yet not wanting to mate with an Earther almost hurts.

Her own breathing slows, and she sighs. "You smell really good for a miner without a bathtub."

Of course I do, since she's picked up the pheromones I'm emitting. "Only for you," I try to joke but am deadly serious. Even if I were born on her world as me, I'd still be appealing to her olfactory senses, but with the bionans running the DNA match sequence for optimal compatibility? She won't be able to resist me. I'm hers, and I need to get G'nar down here now to help me stop this.

"Don't you mean, so do you?" she says, and someone begins yelling outside.

I recognize the voice. Unfortunately, not my Alliance partner but the locked out Gleetar. He has probably just now realized he should have tried harder to find a cave. "He sounds unhappy."

Lin clings to me and whispers, "Oh no, not again."

"What?" Her hands barely meet around my chest, and she's buried her face in my shoulder. I can't begin to think straight with her clinging to me. If I hadn't put on my shirt earlier and blocked a lot of our skin-to-skin contact, my cock would be ready for anything. I find it difficult to focus on anything but overriding the match accepted command. "What's happening?"

Before she can answer, the Gleetar begins shaking the bars to our room and screaming. "I'm not working another fucking shift out here! Open the fucking door!"

Lin scrambles up to stand with feet on either side of my knees. I reach out to pull her closer again. "He can't get in here."

"That doesn't matter." She takes my hands and tries to pull me onto my feet. "We need to go to the back of the room. Now. We're fish in a barrel."

I don't need the Earth idiom translated to guess the meaning. Once on my feet, I shield her bad arm from the others as we all stumble to the far end of the cave. The Gleetar hasn't shut up, and now several are at the bars yelling back at him to go away.

Lin whimpers and sinks to her knees. "Please make it stop," she whispers.

If I weren't so close to her, I'd have missed her plea. A familiar buzzing sound begins. The security bot. I wrap my arms around her, pressing my chest against her back. Thinking about anything but our bodies joined almost hurts. "It's going to get worse, Lin."

"I know."

LIN

"I DON'T THINK THE UNIVERSE's DNA IS GACT BUT FUCK since everyone here knows that word," I say, and Turkh rumbles a low laugh. I more than love how cool to the touch his skin is. His amazing arms are around me and making me feel safe. If my neck and injury didn't hurt so much, I'd relax and fall asleep.

"Some curses just translate better than others."

"The universe is universal. Who knew?" The disc at the base of my skull stops throbbing finally, and I sigh in relief. The painful warning would have ended sooner if one of the frogs had accepted missing out. Now, he and several others are dead. "Maybe now everyone can settle down for the night or whatever this is."

He nuzzles his nose against my hair. I'm sure the smell isn't pleasant, yet, he's treating me like I'm a handful of honeysuckle flowers. "Are you all right?"

"That's what I should be asking you," he says against

my scalp. "We can sleep here." Turkh shifts a little and pulls me up against him as if he's the world's, er, galaxy's sexiest mattress.

I rest my cheek against his chest and put a hand on his bare upper arm. "For a bronze god, you're awfully soft skinned."

"Bronze god?" He lets his lips rest against the top of my head. "I understand the god part, but bronze?"

"It's a type of metal on Earth used for statues and other things." I wish I'd paid better attention in science class and remembered what the mix was so I could tell him. "I don't think it's a pure metal like gold or iron. Do you know what those are?"

He chuckles. "Base element names translate better than a planet-specific mix, yes." Before I can ask him about his home, he asks me, "Are you feeling sleepy yet?" He shifts a little under me. "How's your arm?"

He's deflecting the conversation. Probably isn't an Iron Age graduate on his planet, yet, Turkh's smart enough to leave me thinking they have computers on his world. I can always get answers out of him later when his guard is down, so I follow his misdirection. "I'm crushing you, aren't I?" I try to get up and off him, but he tightens his hold.

"No, you're good. I'm concerned about your injury and how much the translator hurts you."

"Doesn't yours bother you?"

"A little. I have a high pain tolerance and want to know

more about what you experience. What does it do to you when the security system is active?"

"Must be nice," I murmur about his not being racked with pain whenever anyone acts up. He chuckles, and I breathe deep to smell his shirt. I really love his exotic cologne. "My arm is going to sting for a while until it heals. My translator, which I love and hate, only goes haywire when someone starts a fight or fuss. I don't notice it until then."

He runs his fingertips over the back of my neck, and I shiver from the touch. He's warmer than metal despite the metallic sheen, yet so cool under me. Refreshing in this damp hellhole. "Really, it doesn't hurt so much."

"I believe you. I just wish you didn't have one."

"Don't." I yawn as his hand slides down to the middle of my back. "I'd be lost and probably die without it. The trip here was awful because I had no idea what was going on. At least now we have some sort of instruction. Plus, I understand what the other people are saying."

Someone closer to the door stirs before growling, "Shut. Up."

Turkh tenses under me like a cat ready to pounce. I spread my fingers against his chest. "It's all right. He's right," I whisper. "We need to get what sleep we can." He presses his lips against the top of my head and relaxes. I'm not sure how to respond. Is a kiss on his world a sign of romance, affection, or something they give their pets? I don't know and don't want to if the meaning is bad.

My eyes close and the next thing I know, there's noise

and hollering in the distance. It's whatever passes for morning down here. No breakfast or coffee, just a real need to pee. I don't want to open my eyes. Turkh's been here for less than a full day's revolution yet he's already a necessity to me. If only he could run to the surface for snacks, coffee, and my favorite sneakers, he'd be perfect.

"Good morning."

His voice has changed. With my eyes still closed, I can sense the differences a lot better. Somehow, Turkh sounds warmer, more intimate than he did nearly all of yesterday. "No. Not yet."

"You know they'll start spraying us in a little while."

"I know." I lift up and look at his face while the others begin stirring. "We have a little bit of time. Do you mind standing guard so I can, um, eliminate waste?" His eyebrows rise, and I'm sure he's thinking the worst. "I promise it won't be bad. This is the first time I've felt safe enough to ask someone to keep a lookout for me."

His eyes darken in the dimness as he smiles. "I'd be glad to." He lifted his chin. "Let's get started because I want my turn after you."

I get to my feet, every muscle sore. "Huh? You're a healthy guy. You don't need my protection."

"Healthy, huh?" Turkh goes to the back of the room. "Let's stand back here, and the water pressure won't be so bad."

We go to the far wall and wait. The water starts several cells up. Yells from those who don't know the water is cold let me know how close the spray is. The nozzle begins spraying us, and a couple in our group are new, too. Turkh goes to block me, and I move to his side. "No, or I'll miss my chance to get clean."

"Are you sure?"

"Yes."

He moves slowly to let the water hit me, too. I squelch a scream at the icy pain. Hair, face, underarms, privates. I scrub fast to get washing over with before I turn into an icicle. The stream fades to a drizzle. Not helpful when I need to pee like I do. "Okay, we have a couple of minutes to go to the bathroom, uh, waste eliminate, before the room is washed out." I go to a far corner where there's some privacy and put my hands on the top of my pajama pants. "Remember our deal?"

Turkh grins. "Yes," he responds and turns to face the doorway. Other men are peeing against the wall. I drop my drawers and sigh in relief. He chuckles at the sound. I can't say I blame him, but he has no idea. I'm not a country girl. It took me a while to figure out how to do this without making a mess. Guys are so lucky. Done, I pull up my pants and stand in front of him as the other men file out. "Your turn."

"I don't need you to watch out for me."

"Probably not, but it'll keep me feeling useful." I hear him, and the mental image hits me. The guy is pretty tall for the people around here. He'd be an athlete on Earth with his height. I'll bet he's pretty proportional in the package department. I try not to grin, but, it's been a while.

Rick can't rescue me, and I don't think I'll ever see him again.

I'd much rather focus on the man near me. He also needed to pee worse than I did. His holding me all night while I slept gave me the best rest I've had since landing here. A few shouts far up in the mine let me know we don't have much time. "Put a knot in it. Time to go."

He laughs and runs his hands along the walls before looking at them. "I was finished. That'll have to do for washing up."

That was a good idea, so I do the same. The warm rock still holds enough moisture to help me pretend my hands are clean. "I'd suggest waiting until the water comes on again, but you'll lose the top layer of skin." The gates slide open, and the others shove their way out to the corridor. "It only takes once."

"I'll bet." Turkh leads the way to a couple of unused pickaxes before looking up and down the conveyor belt. "So, no breakfast or drink before we start?" He grabs both axes and hands me one of the tools.

"Afraid not." I go to his right and get ready to work. "We'll get our green goo later. There's something in it giving us enough water, but I don't know how." I hit using both hands, and the blow jiggles my arm. The wound kept up the dull ache all night but now throbs with renewed pain. Tears come to my eyes, and I let the ax head fall to the ground. "Damn."

"Let's see," he says and peers down at my arm. I lift the sleeve even if I don't need to. He takes my upper arm in his hand to examine the wound. "I wish we were closer to home. I'd have supplies to help you."

"So do I." A buzzing begins in the back of my neck, and I nod at the wall. "We need to get back to work."

Turkh shakes his head and hits the rock once. "I know." He takes off his shirt and tucks it into his waistband like yesterday. His oddly clean scent hits me again, and I sigh.

When he looks at me, I grin. "Sorry. You're an appealing guy, and I can't help but notice."

"You, um, think so?" He scratches the couple of days' growth of beard on his face. "I mean, am I irresistible to you?"

"Ego much?" I say and chuckle before giving the wall a smack. "When you let me snuggle your cool body yesterday, I realized how alone I've been here." We're both working, and it's odd, but his sweat does all sorts of things to my libido. I take a deep breath and lust curls through me like incense smoke. I turn to him, letting the ax rest for a few seconds. "You also smell so good. Good enough that, yeah, you're irresistible."

He stares at me before leaning in and asking, "You feel this, too?"

So close to me, I can't help but stare deep into his obsidian eyes. The iris seems entirely black until we're nearly nose to nose. Then, I can see the deep blue glimmers in the depths. He's a handsome man. "I do."

Turkh nods before returning to the digging. I watch him for a few seconds before my translator begins tingling. Damn.

All I want to do is spend my time and attention on him. Instead of dragging him back to the now clean room, I begin working with my good arm. He's hitting the wall a little hard, so I ask, "You don't see any sign of the gemstones where we are?"

After a pause, he answers me. "No, not until a few feet into the wall. By that time, well, things change and we may not have to worry about what we hit."

He's right. I may not live long enough to dig so far into the rock. The stone seemed a lot spongier when I first started. I expected the distance between the parallel mine shafts to be a lot narrower by now. Every day it's the same thing, and I'd hoped we'd all make progress enough to get off of this planet by now.

I have to rest every ten strokes or so. Every time I do, I glance at Turkh. He's stoic, working as if he's a machine. I go back to my own digging. If he were mechanical, that'd explain a lot about his skin. Except for the softness. He may look metallic and feel cool, but his skin feels like a rose petal.

Now that I think about it, I'll bet he's not a real person. But then, he isn't a robot, either. They're too primitive, and he's very advanced. I glance at him and can't help but ask, "Hey, Turkh? Are you an android?"

His hits falter as he replies to me. "No, I'm a humanoid. You were there when I pissed."

Him saying "pissed" seems both hilarious and odd. "You know that word?"

"Yes. Another one of those universal words like 'fuck.'"

Okay, "pissed" isn't the oddest word he's ever said. I shake my head and reply, "I guess."

We work a little longer before he says, "Why do you ask if I'm an automaton? Does your planet have them so realistic you can't tell man and machine apart?"

"God, no. Our machines aren't human at all. You have a bronze look to you, your skin is cool, and you're physically amazing."

"You'd mentioned the metal aspect earlier, plus our world is hot. We tend to run cooler than most races."

A hot guy from a hot world. Makes sense. "Are there polar regions on your planet?"

He laughs, and I look at him. As soon as our eyes meet, he shrugs. "Sorry, but every planet has poles. Ours are cool but not enough to turn water into ice."

Amusement colors his words as if the answer were obvious to him. I should have paid more attention in my science classes. Trying to not seem as stupid as he must think I am, I shrug. "Oh, sure. I meant polar ice caps. We have them, and I wondered if everyone did."

As soon as I glance over, he's shaking his head, and that's when I realize the answer is another obvious one to most people. I try to recover by adding, "I mean, not that every world is a ball of ice or even wants to be." After a nagging feeling of digging myself into a deeper hole, I give him a quick grin. "How about you tell me, and I'll stop asking dumb questions."

He stops work to grab my shoulder and give me a

squeeze before resuming work. "They're not dumb. Maybe a little ignorant, but not dumb."

I don't know how to take this and let my pickax fall. "Ignorant, huh?"

"Just your questions seem a little uninformed. Geosciences don't seem to be your society's priority."

"No, you're right. They weren't mine until recently."

He pauses long enough to put a hand on the middle of my back before continuing. "Maybe not, but things always change." I miss when his touch ends. Before I can tell him so, he continues, "I could get into magnetic poles versus rotational axis with a little bit of what happens when either change during a planet or star's lifetime. That's always interesting."

"Um, yeah."

He laughed. "But, I have a feeling you want to know more of the day-to-day events on my homeworld."

"Exactly." I sigh in relief. Geosciences are probably interesting to people, but not to me. "Everything at your home is interesting to me. Where you buy or get food, the vehicles or transportation you have, what you do for fun. Things like that."

The sounds of various humanoids breaking up rock ring out all around us. He seems to think for a while before beginning. "The people at home are united and speak with one voice to other planets. Not that we all agree or even get along with each other. We have conflicts, some heated, but we all gathered together into one society with many cultures eons ago."

"Do you have space flight?"

He's quiet again before answering. "We've made some progress in space travel, yes. A race always wants more no matter where they are."

"I hear that. We started off with our moon before looking at Mars. It's the closest planet to us that isn't 300 degrees or so." I feel rather smart about remembering the surface temperature of Venus, roughly, maybe. Hopefully, because I have no access to the internet to double-check myself.

"Degrees? I assume it's a unit of measurement?"

The tone and mood shift up the mine, distracting me for a moment. "Oh, yes, degrees are temperature or angle things. Math and science weren't my strong points. I'd say in here the air feels like an even one hundred degrees. The dampness makes it worse." I look up the conveyor belt and see the food bin in the distance. "So the other nearby planet to Earth is three times warmer than here. Doesn't sound like much, but it's enough to melt plastic. And me."

My stomach growls, and I can't help but stare as the bin comes closer. We're farther down into the mine, and I'm not sure there'll be anything left. The back of my neck tingles so I keep working. "We're not close to any of the blue stones, are we?"

"Not yet. At this rate, it'll be several weeks."

He sounds as grim as I feel. The food bin rolls closer. Humanoids to my right and up the conveyor begin fighting as the bin approaches. I don't want to admit I know why they're angry. "Shit." At Turkh's questioning expression, I explain, "There are no more food bags by now. For some reason, they didn't make enough for us at the lowest levels."

"What do they have to gain by starving everyone?"

"What do they have to gain by feeding us regularly? The strong survive a day or two without food and save them money or resources while the weak die. It's a win for them both ways." My eyes fill with tears, and the rock wall blurs. "All this won't end until there's nothing left of us or the gemstones." My pickax misses the rock, and the tip crashes into the conveyor belt, jarring my entire body.

Turkh's scent grows stronger, and I want nothing more than to let him hold me until all this fades into nothing, but I can't. We'd both be killed for my weakness. "You said I could never go home again. Did you mean it?"

He's silent for a while with nothing but a slowdown in his work to let me know he's heard my question. "Yes, I did. There's no way you'll ever go back to Earth. Whoever abducted you will get the maximum penalty when they're caught."

His optimism is admirable, but my realism is stronger. "If. If they're caught."

"When they are, not if."

I admire his certainty, but let the argument go. He doesn't know anything more about how the universe works than I do. Bad guys don't get caught. They just pay good guys to look the other way. My stomach growls again. I'm so hungry it hurts, I want a long and hot shower and my car. Not even Rick with his problems and Mom with hers sound bad right now.

For the first time since I was put here, tears roll down my face. Maybe I'm extra dense to have not given up on life by now, but the futility hits me in the gut. I let my ax fall to the floor. "I think I'm done."

Turkh picks up the tool and begins the work for me, alternating with his own. "No, you're not. You're going to stay strong and let me help."

He's sweet, but I don't quite believe he can do anything down here. "For how long? Until you drop dead first?"

"If that's what it takes, yes."

I look over at him. No way can this guy care so much about me in such a short amount of time. Attraction is one thing, but to work himself to death for me? Ha! I reach for the ax. "Okay, I can keep going. Let me have it."

"No."

"Seriously. Let me get back to work."

"No. Take a rest break."

A familiar buzzing begins in my neck, and I reach for the ax. "I need to do my own work because they already suspect something."

He looks at me. "You're getting a signal, too?"

"Yes. They can tell after the first few hours of work when someone has paid another to take over for them." I put my hand on his bicep and hope the touch will sway him. "I'm just upset because I'm hungry is all." I slide down to his now paused hand. "Even with you being right-handed, they've figured out I'm not as strong as you."

He lets me have the ax before taking my chin in his hand. "Promise me you'll believe it when I say you won't die here."

"I..." I do want to believe him. He's certainly strong enough to make things happen. But as the buzzing at the back of my neck grows stronger and begins to hurt, I can't say the words. The hum turns into crackles. I pull away from his touch. A couple of smashes against the stone wall and the pain fades. After a sigh of relief, I tell him, "I'm sorry, but there's no need to lie to each other. We both know I'll die here."

[7]

TURKH

I watch as tears leave clean streaks down her grimy little face. She's the most beautiful person I've ever seen, and her sadness kills me. I can't tell her why I have faith in our escape. I just need her to be strong enough to survive until I get her out of this prison. She's already back to work on the rock, and I say, "Promise me you won't even think about dying here until after I do. Promise me."

"Can I die as soon as you do?"

Her question stabs my heart. She makes me wish for the immortality of a first worlder instead of a limited life span of a second worlder. "Yes. You can only die after I do. Promise?"

"Are promises a big deal for you? As in, you keep them after you make them?"

I frown. Everyone on Ghar treats a promise as sacred. We don't promise anything we can't deliver. I'm not sure how to tell her this without sounding like a Gharian,

79

though. "We do keep them. People have died yet kept their promise afterward. It's a serious task."

"Hmm." She pauses and rubs the back of her neck before continuing. I create a reminder to give her a neck rub and clean her arm's wound after the shift. "We aren't like that on Earth. It's all 'I promise this' and 'I promise that' but nothing ever comes true. I don't go to the zoo with the other kids. I can't borrow the car for a job interview. He works late, so I miss the museum's opening."

She pauses to wipe the sweat from her forehead and leaves a clean streak. The empty food bin goes past us on the belt. We both watch as it disappears before she says, "I mean, it's all okay. I like that you've promised and all, but if something happens and I die here, at least you tried."

My mind stopped at her use of "he," but recording everything afterward gives me an advantage. I want to pry without prying and ask, "So your father or brother didn't take you to a museum?"

"Neither one exists. I mean, I don't know my father, never did, and I don't have a brother. The he I meant is my boyfriend, Rick. He says a lot but, well, you know. Never follows through."

"Boyfriend." The word translates as a young male companion and I hope that's what he is to her.

"Yeah, although he's probably with someone else by now. He's faithful, just not patient." She keeps working while I find it tough to continue. Of course, she had prior relationships. Lin is a beautiful person. Any man would be crazy to pass on getting to know her better. I just don't want anyone else to ever touch her again because she's mine.

Lin's going on about her living arrangements on Earth and what she calls a boy friend. When I stop thinking of ways to ignore my jealousy, I hear her say. "One or two months without sex and he's out hunting for a new roommate."

"Sex?" Her saying the word pulls me from my own thoughts.

She doesn't pause in her litany. "I mean, here I am, not being the most faithful girlfriend by thinking you're hot, but that's different. I'm on another planet and probably the only human here. Meanwhile, he's at home, bored, and probably looking for a new girlfriend."

"Wait, what?" She was intimate with someone, potentially bonded with them? I stop her work with a hand on her shoulder. "You had sex with him?"

She stops and looks at me. "Well, yeah. We were roommates and together." Frowning, she says, "Oh, I see. Is...what planet did you say you're from?"

"I didn't."

"Okay, is this 'Ididnt' a place where you all don't have sex but procreate in test tubes and glass bottles?" She begins working again. "I watched a movie where the people stopped having sex because it was disgusting. Is that what you've done?"

Despite my irritation, I can't help but smile at the idea. We may have one or two unions available to us in our lifetimes, but there are no restrictions on healthy and willing partners. She's giving me the side eye, and I try not to smile. "That's not what *I've* done, no. Others tend to wait until their union before they have sex. I'm not the patient type." She snorts and laughs at the same time. "People are allowed to do what they and their partners want."

"Uh huh. You're acting like my having sex is a big deal while you're over there romancing all the women. I suppose slut shaming is universal, too."

"I don't understand the term."

"It's used to make women ashamed of how many sexual partners they've had. A woman who has slept with a lot of men is called a slut, and there's shame attached."

I really wish the shift was over so I could face Lin and explain my thoughts and meanings behind them. This constant motion and trying to have a conversation at the same time is frustrating. "There are several things I need to communicate to you." After such an opening, I'm suddenly at a loss for words. How can I tell her about our union? About how I don't have a choice and I'm terrified she does? I won't die if she walks away from us, but I'll feel like I don't want to live, either. She's still working, and I glance over at her. Her face is determined as she hits at the rock with one arm. Yesterday's injury on her skin is still red and raw.

She gives me a quick look and grins. "So tell me. My race isn't telepathic, you know."

I laugh. "We aren't either. Sorry, I was thinking." I go back to work and modify my ardor a little bit. "One of the things I need to say is I will never shame you for anything. Your past is done. I only care about now and your future."

"Okay, I like hearing that. Go on."

Her tone is a lot less frosty and leaves me encouraged. "We've both had sex in our life, and I don't care. What we do together in the future is all that counts to me." I stop at a strangled sound from her. "Are you all right?"

"Yeah. Sorry, I had this mental image of us... Anyway, you were saying? More things to communicate, or are you done?"

I don't like lying, even by omission, but it's too soon to tell her we're mates. She's not Gharian. Earthers, especially this one, seem to have sexual issues. Above all, I want to respect her feelings and let her choose me of her own free will. "There's maybe a bit more to let you know." I clear my throat. "You see, we have fun and play around until we meet the love of our lives. It's sort of instant and can happen without warning."

"Oh damn. Sounds like a good idea to me."

I look over, and she's shaking her head. "You don't seem sincere."

Lin bites her lip. "I am. It's just, what if one of you two are already committed to someone else? Do you have three-way relationships?"

I stop mid-stroke at the idea of any other male being with us. Not even another woman appeals to me. I know that's not normal for any male of any race, but I only need her. I clear my throat and try to sound calmer than I feel. "Some do. I wouldn't because I'm too possessive."

"Ah, the jealous type." She stops and leans toward me. I stop, and she bumps our sides together and says, "So am I, so I feel ya."

Our union will work, then. I smile and focus as we both resume the digging. "Good. I don't want to share you with anyone, ever."

"What?"

Her voice comes out at a much higher frequency, and I grin. "I think you heard me. I'm not the sharing kind."

"So you think you have me, huh?" She shakes her head. "Dude, you don't have me to share. We met yesterday. Yeah, I snuggled you because you're literally cool to the touch in this hell hole, but neither one of us is getting out of here alive." I begin to protest, but she holds up her good hand to stop me and continues. "You said I'm not going home and now is not the time for a relationship, remember?"

Certain of how long it'll be before the security bot arrives, I stop working. I face her, taking Lin's available hand to have her stop and turn to me. Her sad eyes melt me, and I want nothing more than to spend the rest of my life making her happy. I let my fingertips trail down to her hand. "Lin, you don't understand. You may not be mine, but I'm all yours. Make no mistake. We're both getting out of here alive. Just because you can't return to Earth doesn't mean we won't be together somewhere else. I can't explain why right now, but neither of us has a choice about our union."

She lets the ax handle fall against her leg and rubs the

back of her neck. "You are a little intense right now about this whole union thing. Why don't we just hang out, work so we're not zapped by the ray guns from the robot, and get to know each other later when we can rest?"

Her sudden coolness hurts. I let her hand fall. Lin picks up her ax and adds, "I can promise you you'll change your mind about me later." She doesn't look at me as she hits the wall. "To know me is not to love me. You'll see."

The effort to not argue with her keeps my teeth gritted from the struggle. My words and meaning were clear, so I go back to work, too. It's easier for me to bust rock until my arms fall off than it is to resist holding her right now. Especially when she sniffs back tears. Pless. "I promise you your faith in me won't be misplaced."

"I'd laugh at that, but you're an Ididnt, right? So you have to live up to your words."

I smile at the mistake I'll have to fix later. Telling her everything about Ghar, taking her home to meet my family, petitioning the Emperor for her citizenship are all things I can't wait to accomplish once the mission is done. "That I am."

We work for a while. I've been focused on her and nothing else. The lull gives me a chance to review what my secondary attention picked up during our prior conversation. I missed a lot, which makes me grateful for the internal recording.

I review the report on what the food the Vahdmoshi serve us is. A plant-based material grown on the surface and enhanced with nutrients and hyper water. I don't smile at the testosterone inhibitors even if it explains a lot about the various behaviors from the long timers here. Just as much as the corporal punishment for slight transgressions keeps the peace, so does limiting aggressive sexual tendencies. G'nar probably shit a charkin when he found out. The guy takes his muscle building seriously.

Which reminds me to compile a report to send when we connect. I set up a notification last night for his signal, but nothing's hit so far. We have enough evidence with Lin's presence alone to convict everyone running the mines. G'nar could signal the director we're done, and the three of us would be off this rock. The lesser worlders would need reconditioning and relocating.

So would Lin. I glance at her without turning my head. The Alliance leaders would strip me of my status if I told her much more than what I have already. They'll dump her and the others here into an eighth world where they're the only sentient life forms. The refugees won't interfere with an emerging race nor will they bring back harmful tech to their own kind. I can't let her go without me.

"I need to go."

I laugh because her thoughts mirror my own too well. "Really? Where to?"

"Somewhere private. I might be thirsty as hell, but my bladder doesn't know it."

"Oh, to piss. Do you have a place in mind?"

"Yeah. One of the opened rooms is good. They're dark, and no one stays there very long."

I nod. The punishment system in the translators is

effective. "All right." I watch as Lin puts down the tool. Before she can walk away, I want to make sure she's safe. "No, don't leave it. Take the pick."

"I don't need to," she says over her shoulder. "No one's bothered me before. The security is too tight."

She's foolhardy, I think, but then I'm probably overprotective. I lose sight of her. She's perhaps found privacy and might appreciate the extra time. I pick up her ax to keep up the illusion she's here. The one-two strokes into the rock give me time to build an argument for Lin staying on Ghar.

But, I can't. She's a sixth worlder full stop. If Earthers had been beyond the orbit of their own moon and could internalize tech, I'd have a stronger case. Otherwise, the leaders might let us live together on a third or fourth world, but there's no way I could bring her home.

I stop. She's been gone a little too long for basic pissing. While she might have good reasons for the delay, I want to be sure she's all right. I put both tools down. Someone talks to me about walking past them, but I ignore the chatter. She went farther into the mine, and I need to find her.

As I walk farther away from our area, men catcall to me about following the tail. I ignore them despite the urge to twist their heads off with my bare hands. No wonder they're down here, useless hunks of meat that they are. Up ahead and on the left, a Blendarian staggers out of an open cave. He's clutching the back of his neck and is bleeding from a gash on his head. His right eye is swollen shut, and I run up to him. "What happened? Did you see an Earther go by here?"

"Who do you think did this to me?" He brushes past me. "I gotta get back to work before this thing kills me."

I grab his arm. "Where is she?"

"Fuck away." He pulls out of my grasp. "Tag her if you want before she dies. I'm done with the little bitch."

A rage engulfs me, and I want to murder this being. "If you've hurt her, I will kill you." I can't tell if he pales. His fur is too thick. He backs away before running up the mine to his place.

I may not have to kill him myself.

My own translator is buzzing, so I know Lin's feeling it, too. Sure enough, I hear her moan among the crush of other sounds around me. She's ahead, so I hurry over and look into the dark room.

Another moan from her, but I don't see her there even after switching to infrared. I hurry to the next open room and see her crumpled against the far wall. "Pless it all!" She displays against the cold rock but barely. "Lin!" I run to her and gather her limp body into my arms. Letting the automatic information retrieval about her condition begin, I hold her close. As cool as she says I am, unlike her, I'm warmer than our surroundings.

She begins struggling, just a little, and I can feel why. The sensor at the back of her neck is sending small electrical shocks. I need to get her out of here before the securbot comes. "Lin, beloved, wake up for me."

"Mm." Her hands push at me. "Stop. Make it stop."

She puts a hand where the translator is and yelps. The damn thing shocked her.

"We've been gone too long." I pick her up. "Come on, sweetheart. I need to get you back to our work area."

"Put me down."

"Not happening."

"I mean it." She struggles in my arms, waking up a little more. "Don't touch the translator. I don't want it to hurt you." I go sideways out of the door, and she asks, "How does it shock my hand but not my neck?"

"Relax. I'll be careful." There's a metal disc on the surface to keep workers from removing it when the punishment starts. Out in the light, her neck is already coloring from where the bastard choked her. I should have killed him when I had the chance. We pass by the Blendarian on our way back, and I kick him onto the conveyor. He scrambles off, and I say, "Sorry," as sincerely as I can. Judging by the glare he's giving me, he doesn't believe me either.

I set Lin down and let her lean against me for a second or two. I pick up our tools, working one at a time. "The next time you need to do anything but work? I'm going with you."

"Okay, unless one of us is on the surface while the other is down here." She reaches for her pick and stumbles into me.

I won't let that happen. If I'm not there, I'll make sure G'nar watches over her instead. She doesn't know about him yet. I'm not sure if I should tell her until I need to do so. She winces, reminding me the translator is still warning her. "Let me work for both of us. A little bit. If the securbot gets here, take your ax back and try to work until it leaves, all right?"

"I will. I mean, I can work now." She reaches for her tool again, but before I can give her the ax, she crumples at my feet.

[8]

LIN

I wake up with a start. There's nothing but darkness. My head and throat hurt like the devil, but I can feel Turkh's cool body against my back. I reach forward to check if the rock wall barely visible is really there. It is.

"How are you feeling?"

His voice, low and gravelly, sends tingles down my spine. The same spine pressed against his chest and stomach. I'd make the joke about a rock and a hard place, except…yeah, he's hard. Despite my headache, I smile. He may be a great guy, but he is a guy. "Sore but fine." He's quiet, too much so, and I'm worried. "What happened?"

"Do you remember the attack?"

His whispers move the hair covering my ears, and I frown because I don't remember much after going to pee. "I remember pulling up my pants before getting hit on the head. Was there more?"

"I wasn't there for the actual attack." His arm pulls me closer. "I found you afterward, unconscious. You woke but fell again." He hesitates before asking, "Where do you hurt?"

I run through everything, tensing muscles everywhere. Even between my legs, just in case the worst happened. "My head and neck mostly. He had his hand on my throat while trying to... Anyway, I kicked him off of me and into the wall." Unarmed self-defense 1 0 1, always use your legs. "How long was I out?"

"Not long. The shift change started when I picked you up. It solved a lot of potential problems for us."

I was out cold after the fox/dog mix of a man went for me. The others could have been next, and unconscious, I'd never be able to fight. I didn't want to use Turkh as a protector until now. Even if we were separated, the mere threat of him killing whoever hurt me might keep me safe.

But am I using him? Really? With him holding me as if I were a treasure, I might be starting to more than like him. Not love, no. Not so soon, and not more than a lusty affection. He hadn't needed to care about me and now for me. Yeah, certainly a little more than like for both of us. "Thank you for saving my life."

"You're welcome. You can sleep. I'll keep you safe until you're feeling better."

What about him? He needs his rest as much as anyone, excellent body or not. Drowsiness means slow reflexes. "I don't want to be a problem for you." I turn my head toward him. "I don't want to get you killed if something happens to me."

"You'll never be a problem, Lin. I care for you."

I could easily fall for him. I turn my body entirely to face him and press my lips against his. His people may not kiss, but saying thank you again didn't seem like enough. He tenses and I pull away a little. I might have crossed some sort of cultural line. "I didn't mean t—"

He kisses me back, making my toes curl. Did I think he was cool? His lips are warm against mine. Apparently, people do kiss where he's from, and it's amazing. He pulls me closer until I have no choice but to feel his cock pressing against my upper thighs.

Turkh smells fantastic. His scent drives me crazy, and it's like fresh soil after rainfall with a hint of mint. There are others in our room, but not many, and I almost want to give them a show when Turkh licks my lips.

"I need to know so I can deal with them," he whispers against my mouth. "Did anyone hurt you since you've been here?"

He pauses before "hurt," and I'm sure I know what he doesn't want to ask. "No. I've always stayed in a group. I've either had an ax in my hand, or the others were too exhausted to try. When they did, I could defend myself." He kisses my forehead as I add, "Today, he jumped me from behind because I was careless."

"I should have been with you."

I run my fingers through his hair, pausing at his stubbly face. The rough texture feels good under my hands. "I don't expect you to be my keeper. Eventually, you'll miss a few too many meals and weaker and weaker." I pause because I can't imagine Turkh ever losing his strength. "If several gang up on you, it's over. And I need to be honest."

He kisses my forehead and says against my skin, "You always have been."

I frown. How can he be sure I've not been lying to him so far? How is he so sure I'm a good person? I can't know if he's decent other than how he's treated me in the past two days. Maybe three. I put my hand on his arm. I'm scared to believe in his goodness. "Then I need to tell you I'm not fooled. I know you're trying to keep my hopes up by insisting we'll be rescued. Hell, you may even believe it's possible, and maybe it is for you."

He's silent for a while. "Your honesty is different from mine."

I sigh because he's not getting it. I see through his efforts. He's not fooling anyone. "Your realistic is different from mine, too." The next part won't be easy because I can already see his irritation in the dim light. "Thing is, you're here, too. If you could have escaped by now, you would have." I can feel anger from the tension in his body. "We both know it," I add, and put my hand on his face. He feels so good against me. I press my lips against his unresponsive ones. "You seem like such a good man, and I'm sure you believe in your plans. I don't mean to ignore what you think." I kiss him again with still no response. He's not happy, and I smile because I have the cure. "I want to make love with you, and we need to find a space and time alone before I die." He inhales sharp enough that I feel his chest press against mine.

"Challenge accepted. I hope you enjoy sex because you're not going to die for a very long time."

I smile. "I suspect sex with you would be out of this world." He laughs, and I ask, "An old one?"

"So old it predates my solar system."

"Older than yo' mamma?" I turn around to face the wall and because I like him spooning me.

He nuzzles my neck. "She's not going to like you aging her so much."

"Now I'm almost glad I won't meet her." When he's quiet, I try to joke with him. "We'll have some sex, some laughs, and you'll hook up with a lovely fox girl they picked up to work here and forget my name."

"Lin?" he says so softly that I have to move closer. "When we make love, it'll be in a place worthy of you. We're getting off of this rock, and I plan on being yours for the rest of our very long lives." I begin to rebut until he puts his index finger over my mouth. "No. There's a lot you can't and don't know right now. The only thing you can be sure of is you won't die here."

He's so sweet and earnest. As soon as his fingertip slips from keeping me quiet, I have to tell him, "I want to believe you, I do, but fighting off that fox man took every ounce of my strength. You helped me today, but what about tomorrow? You look superhuman, but you're not. No one is."

"I would fight to the death for you no matter where you are."

The idea of him dying from one of the others attacking me breaks my heart. I'd have to watch him die before they turned on me. I imagine the worst before saying, "You can't help me when we're separated and I don't expect you to kill yourself in saving me."

TURKH

THERE'S A LOT I CAN'T TELL LIN, BUT I CAN SAY ONE thing. "You don't get to decide what I do when you're in danger. Not now, not ever." I hold her close. "We're not discussing the subject anymore. We've found each other, and I'll be plessed if I'll let anything happen to you."

"Plessed?"

"A curse, doomed, damned, hell. Unique to Ghar." Pless again. I slipped and said my homeworld. If the Vahdmoshi have listening devices in our translators, and why wouldn't they, I've fucked up big time.

"Gar?"

Lin shakes me out of my self-recrimination. She doesn't pronounce her "ha" sounds. Cute, but gar is not my planet and means something entirely different. "Almost like that, yeah. It's a planet." I make a big show of yawning. "Work's going to be here too soon. We should try to sleep."

"Sorry."

97

"Hmmm." I nuzzle her hair, enjoying one last smell of her. "Don't be. I enjoy talking with you, but I need to stay sharp." She's so warm and small. I know her size is deceiving, making me want to protect her physically. Yet, I love the person she is, too, and want to keep her safe mentally as well. "Goodnight."

"Goodnight."

The next morning, my internal sensors wake me before I truly come to. They're picking up irregular voices, and I stir. Only, Lin's snuggled next to me. I don't want to disturb her. Not until the showers are closer.

Just when I'm about to rouse her from sleep, she moans and sits up. "That has got to be the worst alarm clock in the world.

I chuckle as others groan and get to their feet around us. "Could be worse. They could just start with hosing down the room."

"You're right." She lets me help her up and smiles. "I didn't know you were such an optimist."

"Give me a few sas, and you'll know everything about me."

"Sass?" The water begins and she yelps. "Yikes! I'd hoped it would be warmer than this." She began scrubbing as if soaped. "We either get chilled water or food but not both."

I watch her and half-heartedly wash myself. Since I never think to look anywhere but her beautiful face, I'm now noticing how torn her clothes are. The fabric is a plant and plastic mix of fibers. I can tell where the weak spots are on the knees and inner thighs.

"What?"

I glance up at her. "Nothing. I was just thinking about a real shower."

"God, me too. Every minute of every day."

When we are back on Ghar, I'm having a buffet delivered every day. She can relax in a tub of whatever temperature of water she wants, and I'll feed her myself. The daydream helps me ignore the spray. The spray slows to a trickle as the doors slide open. People begin leaving the room. Lin is wringing the water out of her hair as I watch.

She takes my hand and pulls me out into the mineshaft. I give her fingertips a squeeze before letting go. "Thank you. You'll have to tell me what a fire hose is. I forgot to ask yesterday." Before the gates clang shut, a stronger blast of water cleans out the rooms. Lin's right. I do not want to be caught in there after the gentle shower is finished.

She grins and picks up a pickax, giving it to me. "Sure, as soon as you explain sass to me."

I take the tool and can't help but return her amazing smile. "Sas, short on the ess, is my planet's rotation around our sun."

"Ah, a year."

After pulling up Earth's statistics, I run the math. "Nearly. Our sas, equal to your year, is three hundred and twenty of your days long."

"A shorter year with more frequent birthdays and holidays? Hell yeah. Or is that pless yeah?"

I need to warn her about using "pless" too often. It's actually not for polite company, and my mother would be horrified if Lin said the word in front of her. "Um, something like that."

"How old am I on your world? How old would you be on mine?"

Her enthusiasm is fun, and I need to know more. "How old are you on yours?"

"Twenty-seven."

"All right." I watch her use both arms with the tool. She's feeling better, thankfully. "Doing the math, considering we have twenty-five-hour days, you'd be around twenty-nine, maybe thirty."

"No!" She laughs and shakes her head. "I can't be that old. We're living on Earth no matter what, unless..." She pauses for a moment to look at me. "Unless we can live somewhere and I'm younger there."

"Do you want a planet with air or no air?"

"The key words are 'live on.'"

"Ah, a solid surface planet with an atmosphere and temperate climate means I'd have to find a planet circling a huge star."

"The longer it takes, the younger I am, right?"

"You know longer is always better," I can't help but quip and laugh when she gasps. Lin is perfect no matter how old she is, and I say, "Don't worry about your age. Thirty isn't bad at all. I'd be thirty-two on Earth."

"So you're how old on your planet?"

"Thirty-five." Because I need to impress her, I ignore my orders to be quiet about anything beyond sixth world and add, "I'm rather young to be an Enforcer. Most people my age are still Protectors."

"Very good. I'm a store clerk, and most people my age are successful."

Her tone leads me to believe she's being sarcastic or at least wry. I'm not sure what "clerk" means. The translator is using her word, not mine. With "store" in front of it, I think she's a Helper. "You help people in stores with what they need?"

"Exactly that."

"You'd do well on my planet. Helpers are a valued group of workers."

"As much as Enforcers?"

I repeat the phrase drummed into us as soon as we're old enough to understand. "Everyone has their place, and every place is important." I stop work as a sound I've been hearing grows louder. "How is your arm? Can you hit on both your rock and mine for a little while?"

"Sure? Bathroom break?"

"No, dinnertime."

"So soon? Doesn't matter, just bring me back some dessert."

I laugh and head up the mine shaft. The food bin is far enough ahead to be more than half full, and if I jog, I'll get there in time to grab several bags. As I approach, I can see there is a fight of sorts. Everyone else has had the same idea due to yesterday's shortage. After a quick check of who's there, the fucker who attacked Lin is still not around. I push my way through and reach in for my own handful of bags. A sharp pain stings my forearm. I yelp and pull back my hand. There's a bite mark on my skin with some punctures deeper than others.

The bite aches and I shove aside who I think did it. I grab several more food packets before pushing my way back out of the crush. Just in time, too, because a securbot is flying toward us. I ease away and walk back to Lin as the fuss dies in the bot's whirring arrival. Others grab at my food but are easily deflected by my elbows.

As I approach, Lin turns to me and smiles a little before seeing how much I'm carrying. "Wow! You weren't kidding."

She runs up to me, and I give her a food parcel to start with. She stops cold and stares at my forearm. "What the hell happened? Someone bit you."

"Weird, don't you think, since I'm neither green nor liquid."

Taking my arm, she examines the wound. "What if it gets infected?"

Not a chance, thanks to my bionans. "I have a strong immune system and this food"—I hold up a food pack—"has a touch of medicines."

"I'd ask if it's safe to eat, but it's been a month or so, and I'm not dead yet."

While shoving a couple into each pants pocket, I

watch her eat. One of the packs is empty, and I give her another one with a grin. "You make the goo look good."

"Sorry to be so rude but I'm starving." She goes back to eating before adding, "Are you going to have anything?"

"I will." I should probably act desperate. The bionans were programmed to expect the mission might require long stretches without nourishment. I forgot to act hungry at appropriate times. "Yeah, it's one of those so hungry I'm ill feelings."

"I felt that way the last time I missed the food bin." She drinks more of her dinner. "I've lost weight since then." I examine her up and down before turning on the schematics to see what she'd look like with extra weight. She crosses her body with one arm. "Hey, no imagining me fatter, buddy. I kinda like being this slender for a change."

"It's good to know women are the same all over the galaxy."

"Don't tell me we're expected to be skinny on other planets, too."

"Not skinny as much as conscious of your appearance." I finish up with my meal. "We all are. It's part of our programming to appeal to potential mates."

A thin sheen of sweat glistens across her skin. Her coloring keeps me fascinated with its vibrancy. The way her body moves also has me staring more than anything else. She's beautiful but has this completely unaffected air as if her world had no reflective surfaces. She crumples up the food pack and tosses it aside. "I'd hoped the advanced civilizations would be above biology and the need to please others."

My body was wise to choose her as my match. She grins and glances away, and I realize I've been staring at her like a boy around his first love. "Sorry, you're a little distracting." Her face turns pink, and I rush in to address her statement about higher worlds and lower instincts. "Anyway, no matter how much we learn, our predispositions are animal. Which animal depends on what planet you're from. But yeah, the need to appeal to someone special and please them physically is true for everyone."

"Good to know I'll fit in somewhere. I don't want to be the continually dumb one if I leave." Before I can rebut her, she winces and shakes her head. "Damn, this hurts. I need to get back to work before the pain gets worse." She picks up her ax and hits the rock wall. "How is it you can stroll all over for food yet not feel the translator trying to kill you?"

As she's working, I pick up my ax, too. I can't tell her about the bionans, of course. "It does. I just have a high pain tolerance." I hit the wall, too, for emphasis. "The work helps. I just pretend I'm bashing on whoever took both of us."

"I've been imagining Mr. Fox from yesterday. I'm glad you're here, too, because I can barely tell them apart." She leans closer to me. "He could be a couple of people down, and I wouldn't know it."

I would. "Don't worry. I've watched for him, and he's

nowhere around."

"How could he leave his work area without the robots gunning him down?"

"Good question. Maybe he ran off far enough to be eliminated without us hearing him. Doesn't matter. As long as he's far from you, I don't care." One of the Gleetars is staring at us, and I glare at him. "Anyone who even looks at you will answer to me."

Lin isn't even paying attention as the Blendarian works a little more intensely next to her. "That's really good to know." She picks up a chunk of rock, which fell at her feet, and tosses it on the conveyor belt. "If there's anything I can do for you in return, just say the word, and it's done."

The Blendarian snorts. "I know what I'd like. Care to let me protect you?"

I pause in my work and turn toward him with the ax. "Touch her and die."

"Fine, no touching." His wide, thin lips turn up in a hideous smile. "Let me watch when she pays you?"

"She doesn't exist to you, buddy." I step closer to him and growl, "You don't watch, you don't talk, and you sure as pless don't touch. Got it?"

Muttering something I'm sure is a curse in his language, he returns to busting rock. Lin leans closer to me. "Thanks, again. He's right, though. Sex is probably the only way I can pay you f—"

"Stop." Yes, I'm saying this more to me than her because my dick is already starting to stir at the images crowding my brain. "You can pay me back by staying out of trouble and by being my friend."

"Ow, friendzoned by a luscious Greek god. Yer killin' me, man."

She's grinning at me, so the tone doesn't match the words at all. "Friendzoned" doesn't translate except as a friend in an area. "Luscious" does, and I know my face is darkening from the rush of blood. Embarrassment affects a lot of species, including mine. "Just, no. I don't mean to put you in a friends area, but I don't want you to owe me in that way, either."

"Not even a little?"

Lin's smile lets me know she's teasing, I think. "A lot, but not in debt repayment."

"Oh."

She's quiet for a while. Even though I want to know everything she's thinking, a system notification lets me know I have maintenance to do. All of my focus, biological and mechanical, has been on Lin and not on my mission. Thank the Origins for my peripheral senses. Otherwise, the director and G'nar would gang up to kick my butt back to Protector status.

Sorting through the input doesn't take long. I leave in some of the time I held Lin, but very little. After marking it "Personal," I move the data to private. The information could be requested, and if the Leaders become involved, I'd have to turn it over to them. Let's hope they consider the information mundane enough to ignore.

Lin would need to know about everything I am and

where I'm from before we became close. I'd want to inform her that anything intimate could be viewed by everyone in my command chain. After a glance at her, she seems as into her own thoughts as I am. I've recorded everything down here. The systems, the lack of guards, and the hot damp smell. Even now when I test the air, my stomach churns. No wonder a bag of goop a day is good enough for most of us. I ask Lin, "Does it smell bad in here to you?"

"Bad? No, worse than bad. Like someone's butt after they've wiped with a dirty gym sock and eaten fish."

"A rectum wiped with an unclean athletic foot covering from someone who's ingested an aquatic creature?" I glance at the Blendarian who's standing past two Gleetars to Lin's left. "You're right. That's exactly the smell."

She stops work long enough to nudge into me. "That's so bad! Does the frog men know they're aquatic?"

"It's something they don't like to think about since their ancestors and sentient distant cousins still breathe water. In fact, water-breather is an insult to them."

"Good to know. I suppose if your distant cousins were primitive water-breathers, you'd want to forget you were related."

"Exactly." She goes back to work, this time with a slight smile. I need to get her out of here. Hell, get G'nar and us out of here, and back on Ghar, but especially Lin. She deserves better than this hellhole.

I run through our escape plans, adding her as a variable. None of them work. She doesn't have the speed to keep up with G'nar and me. The delay she causes dooms our efforts every time. I refuse to accept the results and start changing the parameters in trial after trial.

The three of us, her and me, and G'nar and her, are all possibilities for us escaping. Yet, our only option for success seems to be when we leave her here. I even try that scenario and hate the results because G'nar and I escape. If she's alive by the time I can come back for her, the Alliance will insist she go to a lesser world. A fifth world, probably, since the lesser ones would view her as an advanced being to curry favor with at best or abuse for her power at worst.

No. She and I will both stay on a second world. I have the bionans and knew when I accepted them I'd be trapped at a first or second world level. Anything lesser is too dangerous anywhere else. Even the most primitive of nanites have been weaponized by worlds and left void of life as a result. There's no way I could do that to Lin's planet or any other.

Her work rhythm slows, and I glance at her. "Everything all right?"

"Yeah." She rubs her neck with one hand and hangs on to the ax with the other. "I want a bathroom break but can't decide if it's worth going."

"Why?"

"By the time I find a place private enough, the pain from this little bitch is unbearable." She lets the ax fall but doesn't stop trying to massage her neck. "Too bad there's not some sort of deactivation code on this thing."

I'm an idiot. The solution has been in front of me the

entire time. If she has the latest in nanotechnology via my biological nanites, the Alliance will have no choice. She'll either live on a planet with nanotech or be banished to an eighth world of no sentient life. To prevent the exile, I could cement our bond and accept our union fully. Between the bond and tech, I'd be backing the Alliance into a corner.

Except.

I'd be backing Lin into a corner, too. No, I'd want her to join me willingly. I'll quickly program some basic bionans to deactivate the punishment measures on her translator. Just an overwrite so the Vahdmoshi can't punish her for long bathroom breaks. We'll need a few seconds alone for the tech transfer. "Come on. I'll go with you."

"You can't watch me every second and besides, privacy."

I grin, sure as to why she wouldn't want me there for this type of break. "Usually, I'd agree, but this time I have a solution for the pain. As soon as I'm done, you're on your own for a while."

"All right." She let her ax fall. "Follow me."

Of course, I do, watching that adorable butt of hers as she leads me on. Various men watch her walk by. I want to laugh at the glares they give me. I'd hate me, too, if I didn't have a woman like Lin to care for. She looks back at me with a slight smile. "This looks good."

She ducks inside, and I join her. Her alluring scent distracts me, and I take a step forward until we almost touch. She's lovelier in visible light, so I turn up the photoreceptors instead of switching to infrared.

I lean forward to kiss her, and she puts her hands on my chest. "Easy there. I was promised a solution to the neck pain. Fix it, and I'll owe you more than one."

She's right. I want the nanites to go to the translator, not to her. A kiss would place them in the wrong system. "Sorry, I'll have to be behind you."

"Ooh, kinky."

"Really? Seems rather ordinary to me," I chide, and her snort of a laugh makes me laugh, too. "Lift your hair from your neck and hold still for a moment." After I gather all of the programmed nanos to the tip of my tongue, I lick her translator. They're all transferred and working their magic. "It should happen fast, relatively speaking, and you won't feel anything from the device other than a vague tingling when the security has been called. So you'll need to pay attention for the securbots and react as if everything is normal. Otherwise, they'll get suspicious." She lets her hair go, and I regret not stealing a kiss on her neck while I had the chance. "Also, I didn't deactivate the tracking program because doing so would trip an alarm system. I'll have to work on it later and provide an update."

"Turkh, I don't understand a word you just said." She turns to face me. "Did you short circuit this? But how and how much time do I have before it resumes operations? Shit. They'll know about the malfunction and probably blame me." She starts pushing me out of the room. "If you can understand me, stand guard, but not too close, and I'll be done in a couple of minutes. Go back if your translator starts hurting you."

"I will. Go on and do your business."

"Gah! Still nothing. I'm gonna have to learn a new language." Her voice fades as she goes farther into the cave. "Damn it, languages because I'm doomed without this thing. Damn it all to hell."

The nanos are reprogramming from the base code up. I know she'll understand me by the time she's done. I don't want to laugh at her distant grumbling and an occasional curse, but it's rather cute. We're in deep trouble, but now I know we're in this together.

She's quiet now. Too quiet. I wait a few seconds more before calling back to her. "Lin? Are you all right?"

"I think so." I hear her wet footsteps as she comes back. "My neck doesn't hurt, my arm feels great, and I can understand your Gharian." Her eyes widen. "I even know what Gharian means. Now that I know about the Alliance and your role in it, I need more answers from you. What the hell did you do to me?"

[10]

LIN

THIS. IS. AMAZING. I KNOW SO MUCH MORE, NOW. I can even do math and know what a quadratic equation is for. Still end my sentences on a preposition, but so what? I can relearn grammar later. I stop and stare at Turkh in the dark room. Correct that. I can learn ALL the grammar from ALL the languages. "You gave me information."

"I did?"

"You've given me the universe." He looks panicked, and I hold up a hand. "No, you just gave me the galaxy, but still. It's a hell of a lot." My neck begins tingling, almost a tickle, and I laugh. "We need to get back to work, don't we? How funny." I give Turkh a kiss before I walk past him. "Let's go."

I look at everything around us with fresh eyes. We're in a mine of metamorphic rock and digging for proth. Ha! Everything has a name. We're surrounded by Blendarians, Gleetars, MoNse, and Mwrarns, and I can't help but laugh

113

again. I know Turkh is a Gharian from Ghar, where the nanos were made. I have nanos! How very futuristic! I'll have to see if they're permanent or sadly temporary because I want these babies for forever.

And Earth? I search the database for home. Turns out, I'm a sixth worlder, two rungs up from the bottom of the heap. Yikes! I'm forbidden. While Turkh is picking up his ax, I tease him. "Hey, you're not supposed to be messing around with me. I'm a mangy sixth worlder, you know."

He sighs before answering. "I know. It's a problem I need to solve."

"Wait. You *want* to mess around with me? Nice!" The more I learn about him, his world, the Intergalactic Alliance, the more I realize his status in the galaxy. No wonder he seemed cranky when we first met. He liked me even then. "You know where I'm from, right?"

"Yes. Our bond is a serious problem that I'm not sure how to fix at the moment."

The punishments I can pull up confirm his words. The word "bond" triggers a display of "see also" in my mind. I can push it off until later, create a task list, start a countdown timer. It's like having a smartphone times a thousand in my brain. No wonder he seems distracted sometimes. He's doing some amazing thinking. "Yeah, I'm sorry about that. I had no idea of what being friends with you could do..." I let my words trail off because he's not here for fun. My bet is a covert job of sorts, and I don't want to jeopardize anything else for him. Beyond the current messing around with a sixth worlder problem he currently has. "We should probably not speak to each other anymore. Stop being friends."

"Sure. We can start now because being without you would be so easy." He gives me a grin. "I'll even let you walk away first."

He is so full of it. While he was teasing me, I looked up relationship topics on his homeworld. There's a biological matching based on DNA compatibility. How our two races match up is a whole 'nother rabbit hole of information I'm dying to go down, but later. Because, it seems there's a match, acceptance, then union and the Gharians don't play around. Their unions are for life. I'm sure mistakes can be made, but from what I'm learning, the pairings are deeply biological.

"You're too quiet."

And he's too observant. I can't help but smile. "I'm... thinking." Super thinking, which is super fun. I need to thank him for this gift. "You know, what you did back there? It's amazing. There's a whole universe of information, and all I have to do is want to learn."

"I gave you too much."

I can't deny what I've learned about the Intergalactic Alliance so far. "Yeah, you did. We're gonna fry for this." Maybe not fry so much as be banished to something less than Turkh's second world. Hell, even a fifth world would be pretty damn impressive to me. A place where people missing limbs could regrow new ones? I could do so much more for my people with such technology.

Which is probably why I'm forbidden to go home.

When he'd said I would never return, I figured he meant I'd die here. I look over at him to see him staring at me. I can read his micro expressions. Ah, it's how he knew I never bothered to lie to him. He's a human, er, humanoid lie detector. Still, he's off-the-charts concerned. I want to comfort him and send a feeling type of thought to him. *It's okay, Turkh. I can hide this from the others.* The words have an odd echo as I push them to him.

He falters, letting the ax head fall to the conveyor belt. *Pless it all to hell.*

I hear his words in his voice. Before I can think anything else to him, he turns back and begins working again. *Just wait until we run into G'nar. He'll pull off my arms, and I'll deserve it.*

I'm a little bit horrified but am not getting the same feeling from him. He must be exaggerating. *Pull off your arms? That seems a bit brutal. Have him just kick your ass instead.*

Just a kick?

I hope it's the same concept of only beating you up. Otherwise... I glance at his biceps as he works. *Losing those babies would be a damn shame. You're fine.*

He laughs and gives me a grin. *While I should have had better control of the nanos, I rather like this.*

Me too. This whole intracranial communications thing, innercoms for short, are terrific. Kind of like earbuds, only better because there's nothing to lose in your car or purse. Hearing his voice in my head is a comfortably intimate feeling. Instead of his words caressing my ears, they're hugging my heart.

We need to communicate aloud from now on. No more using the intracranial comm.

Are you sure? This is the ultimate in secret languages.

"I am, because we'll slip up and use it around G'har. He'll know what I've done and honestly? The fewer people who know, the better."

As I open my mouth to ask what's the worst that could happen, my new functionality answers me. Exile to a prison planet. "You bet. No one will ever find out from me." I say this, then thinking about how cool all this new information is, add, "Except, I like learning a ton more, and the no-pain thing is great, too."

"Good. If we don't alert anyone to your additions, we should be fine."

No sooner do the words leave his mouth than the whistleish sirens begin. I try to grin at his piercing glare. "Sounds like an early shift change. It's nothing I've done."

"Uh huh. I hope you're right." He follows the others' example by dropping the pickax and facing me.

People around us are chattering. I can understand the different languages as they speculate on what's happening. It's interesting now that additional facts about each species pop up in my mind. Now I really want to explore the entire galaxy and see what happens. I smile at Turkh. Or, I could hang out with him and study his body. His shirt is dirty. I let my eyes trail a little farther south. Pants, too, could use a good scrubbing.

Before I can get lost in fantasies about bubble baths, there's some shuffling deeper into the mine. People to our far left have started making the trip down before being turned around at the end and coming back to the surface. It'll take a while before those in the exiting side actually leave the work area. I sort of want to tell Turkh via the link but don't want to irritate him. Especially when I can feel the concern almost radiate off him like body heat. "I know our reshuffle between surface and underground is about a month or so early." The number flashes in my mind, and I smile. "Or, an eleventh of a sas."

He gives me a slight grin because I haven't dragged out the final ess. "Good. I'll feel better when we're back to mining, and nothing else is going on."

So will I. Now that he's planted the idea in my mind, I wonder if the nanos are the reason behind the early shuffle. Or if the shuffle is even happening. Turkh nods and I turn around to see the guy to my left walking. I follow him, and Turkh follows me.

I can't help but fret. What if it's a full-scale removal of everyone here? It's been a full day since anyone found a piece of proth. My heart leaps into my throat. What will they do with us? Not transport us home. Leave us here? Execute us? Turkh and G'nar have an escape plan, but I don't. I can feel my pulse in my fingertips and almost jump out of my skin when Turkh puts his hands on my shoulders and leans forward to say in my ear, "Stop. Whatever happens, I'll be there for you."

"Can you be? You have a mission, and I'm not a part of it."

I feel his lips against my hair as he quietly says, "As long as I'm alive, beloved. I'm here."

Love and warmth flood me. Not all of the feelings are from me, and I realize they can communicate with more than just words. Sending emotions, huh? This could be fun. When my mind turns to the sexy, and I imagine stripping Turkh in slo-mo, I hear his laughing aloud before I turn to him. "Merely a couple of ideas for later."

"Good. Looking forward to them."

We turn and head uphill to the entrance. It's stop and go with each step, each one making me a little more nervous. Turkh's anxiety is climbing like a physical force behind me. I'd like to reassure him about changing so soon, but I can't. The men here either ignored or tried to hustle me.

As I near the opening, the mineshaft has grown broader and cooler. Every so often, a gust of air flows down the mine, and I shiver from the cold. I always need a few minutes to warm up from the heated lower levels. I want to talk with Turkh using my voice but am afraid of ruining his cover. *Turkh? If this is like last time, they've brought in new people, and we might be able to link up with your friend.*

"He's more my partner."

"Oh, shit."

After a chuckle, he says, "No, not like that sort of partner. And no using the nanos from now until I say we can. If our innercom tripped up security, we need to stop before we started."

"Are you two the only ones here? And how did they not notice you're slumming it with us?"

He focuses on something distant and gives a nod. "We are, and the systems around here are automated enough to let us pass. We also have the upgrade in nanotechnology, biological nanites, since current tech scans for inorganic versions."

Two kinds? Now I need to know how powerful the new type is. "Are you sure I can't access the information about them right now?"

"Yes. Do it later when we're safe in the mine or in the fields." Turkh takes my hand. "Let's go."

He's warm in the cold air. His muscles are tense from the situation and the environment. Nice, and I want to press against him for more than the obvious reason. The talking from everyone here echoes off of the smooth walls. The large gathering area is the most crowded I've ever seen. With the nanos' help in identifying the various races of humanoids, it's as if the entire galaxy has picked here for a galactic convention.

Like Kim and her four-leaf clover ability, I spot someone ahead of us who looks a lot like Turkh in size and coloring. Only, his hair is lighter and his skin is darker. He's otherwise as metallic, muscular, and menacingly tall. I try not to smile at the idea of being the filling in a man sandwich. Good idea, me being the white cheese between two whole wheat hunks.

"Stop that."

"Sorry, but you're both fine as hell." A rare type of person for here, Khscc, formerly known as Mr. Lizard, blocks my view. I follow Turkh out from around him and to the other Gharian in the building. I didn't think it was possible, but the man is taller than my guy.

He looks from Turkh to me and back. "Plessing Tunsa. You gave bionans to an Earther?"

Tunsa? Ah, he means hell or something similar. When these two stop broadcasting fury at each other, I'll need to look up their idea of heaven. Plus, these bionans are somewhat uncontrollable. As soon as they think I need something, they're on it. I have no idea how to shut them down as much as Turkh wants me to.

Turkh leans toward the other Gharian to hiss, "Just the base ones."

"Doesn't matter. You're dead meat."

11

LIN

I REALLY DON'T CARE FOR THIS GUY ACTING LIKE HE'S Turkh's boss, because as far I know, partner is equal. Not superior. "Excuse me? He did what he had to in order to keep me safe."

The Gharian holds up a hand. "Hush, Earther. The grownups are talking."

Rage fills me, and I don't need any advanced tech to broadcast it. "Fine. I'm out." I turn on my heel and leave. No, I don't know where to, exactly, but away from the both of them.

I glance back. They're talking, and Turkh's back is ramrod straight. He's not happy. Good. I like it when we match up in emotions. Other workers jostle me. One young man comes up and asks what's going on. He's somewhat clean, so I know he's new. Plus, he's a lovely shade of lilac with light hair to match. I'd bet he has purple blood. "You're in a mining colony." He shakes his head, and I twist him to see he hasn't been given a translator yet. I shrug like I don't know anything because telling him anything wouldn't do any good. Plus, my bet is he came up through the avian branch with thin bones. Strong, yes, as in, able-to-break-endurance-records-in-cardio-stuff strong, but not mining-for-fuel strong.

A fight breaks out to my far right, near the entrance to the translator tube. While I seem to be far enough away for safety, I don't want to take a chance. I hurry back to Turkh and... The bionans supply me with G'nar. Great. Anyway, just because one of them is a jerk doesn't mean I need to deprive myself of the other.

Sure enough, the lasers begin, followed by screams, and finally cries for help. The three of us don't say anything at first until G'nar shuffles his feet and says to me, "You might not be aware of how much trouble you both are in with the Alliance. Turkh's given up his career, and I don't know what they'll do with you."

"G'nar," Turkh breaks in. "Enough."

"I'm just honest."

He is. After scanning his micro expressions, I sense more angry frustration than malice, arrogance, or even irritation. He and my guy are good friends, and I respect his concern. I also need to pronounce his name like an Earther and not like an Earther with the galaxy's database in her head. "Thank you, Gunnar."

He raises an eyebrow and looks at Turkh, who shrugs. "She's not accessing the bionans until we find out why they called us up here."

Shit. I can't tell him none of us have a choice because the bionans are accessing me.

"Good." G'nar faces me again. "How much have they changed in you so far?"

"Ahh," I try to begin. G'nar will know I'm lying if I even think about fibbing. "Probably too much. I can use an innercom with Turkh, can translate anything, and have access to so much information." A look passes between the men. "What?"

"How much programming did you give her bionans exactly," he asks Turkh. "Did you intend to give her so much functionality and access?"

"All I wanted was for the translator they installed to stop hurting her. Nothing more. It was supposed to be a closed subroutine to mute the nerves around the device while keeping the tracker inside."

He nodded and scratched his forehead for a couple of seconds. "That should have been all it took."

"But the bionans."

"Yep. I haven't had a chance to go through their programming, either, and if you gave it to her quick and dirty?"

I can't help but snicker. G'nar's frosty gray eyes narrow while Turkh's warm black ones shine. "Sorry. It's an Earth saying and never mind."

"Like I'd mentioned, if you didn't go over every line of code, there's no telling what the bionans are doing to her."

Before Turkh can rebut, the signal to line up sounds and we're being herded to the translator tube and divider between mines and fields. I take his hand. "They had every other person go to the mine both times. Maybe we should put Gunnar in between us."

Turkh shakes his head. "It's Guh-nar, and from what I'm seeing, they're doing something different this time."

He's right. I'm too short to see the breakdown, though. "All right, we can divide up however they're sorting us. I don't want to be alone again."

"You won't be." He leans against me. "We'll work it out." I want to take his hand, but G'nar is looking at us as if memorizing every detail. Instead, I just nod and let them herd us closer to the division area. The tube doesn't come down for those with translators. I try to see ahead. Turkh stands on tiptoes and says back to G'nar, "Looks like they're going in threes this time.

"Count back to us?"

Turkh squeezes my hand and says, "Yeah. You up or down?"

"Doesn't matter. Wherever you two are."

"Which would you want, G'nar?" he asks.

G'nar shrugs, not looking away from the two doorways. "Planetside is colder than in here, but the ground is warm. We're planting, weeding, or harvesting all the time and the heat rises from the soil." He shrugged. "I don't mind working the fields."

Turkh counts ahead. "All right. Let one ahead of us to make it happen."

G'nar steps back to allow someone to go ahead of us and I feel like I've been watching a tennis tournament or ping pong match. "I wouldn't mind losing the chance of accidentally hitting proth ore."

"That's another thing." Turkh turns to G'nar. "The proth is running out in our area already. It's been hours since anyone found something while digging. I don't see anything in the rock, either."

G'nar nods. "When they figure it out, I don't know if they're going to start another mine or pick up from here to go somewhere else."

I'm not sure I want to hear the answer but have to ask. "What happens if they discover you two are here and, you know, don't belong?" Turkh frowns at me, letting me know he caught my meaning without my having to say "Alliance" and "investigation."

He puts a hand on my shoulder and pulls me closer as G'nar answers, "Generally, the lead Vahdmoshi executes everyone and lets the guards go to the next assignment."

An execution? Not good because here and now would be a great place to zap us all with their roving security bots. I look up, and there are several of the little bastards zipping around. We're easy prey. I swallow the rising bile. "Everyone? They can't just recycle us for some other shady business?"

A look passes between the men before Turkh says, "Usually, the workers are too weak to survive the trip to another planet. Killing them also leaves no witnesses behind for the recently finished crime."

"I refuse to believe you all don't have better gathering techniques. What about fingerprints, fibers, metal alloys?

Paint chips? Come on. Stuff a goo packet in your pocket and let's go find evidence for a conviction."

"Goo packet?" G'nar looks ahead of us. I hadn't noticed how close we are to the separation point. "Never mind. We're in a weak spot in the signal blocking mechanism. Before anything else happens, we need to let the Alliance know what we've found."

"Have you been able to break through while out in the fields?" Turkh asks.

"Some but not a lot. I can transmit a sentence or two, get an answer, then the channel goes dark."

We're maybe twenty people away from being shuttled to the mines or the fields. I don't want to access the database in my head to double-check, but I'm pretty sure we could be near an antenna or cell tower device now as a team. "The three of us together would boost the signal."

G'nar shoots me down. "No. They'd notice the transmission, and we couldn't be sure our message would be received by the director."

I step between the men as the last six people before us line up. "We have to try. The message won't go out for sure if we chicken out."

"Chicken out?" G'nar frowns and addresses Turkh. "Do you...?"

"No idea."

Nothing is familiar around here, so you'd think I'd remember to keep down the slang. Yet I keep forgetting not everyone is familiar with the random idioms I use. I don't think people even register how many of them they'll use in a day unless shoved into an English as a second language situation. I sigh and rub my sweaty palms on my pajama pants. Last time I went through this process, some new guy attacked me. Turkh took care of my arm but can't stop the nightmares. As we edge closer to the dividing area, I can hear the announcement better.

"Keep calm and accept your assignment. All upsets will be corporally punitive."

I want to grab Turkh's hand for comfort but don't. I can relax once we're together on the surface or underground. G'nar goes through the translator tube. It gives him a pass. Turkh's through, and I'm up next. I also go through, a little breathless from holding my breath in fear until now. His bionans did the job correctly if not a little overzealously.

We're approaching the two doors. I'm nervous about being on the surface. What if the cold is unbearable? I didn't wear socks to bed that night. I don't want to lose a toe to frostbite. But then, G'nar looks okay. I didn't think to check his fingers and toes to see if any were missing.

Turkh turns to me. "We're up in a few seconds. No matter what happens, stay with me." I nod, my throat clogging up from the urge to cry. "You'll be fine."

I count as people are directed to their next work area. Right, right, right. Now three men are ahead of G'nar. Left, left, left, and we're next. Three rights and I follow the Gharian men out to the planet surface.

We move with the others onto a concrete slab. A securbot hovers above a round metal container full of bags.

People reach in for the silver plastic and walk away. As we draw closer, the announcement here is different from either the main room or the mines.

"Take five bags. Take one row. Fill bags with fruit. Leave bags and debris in row for pickup."

The landscape was more colorful the evening I'd arrived. The sunset, maybe sunrise now that I think about it, gave everything a beautiful glow. Row after row of plants are to our left, and everyone meanders over to them. I'm glad we're up here despite the chill in the air. In the midday, the flat lighting gives everything a dull appearance. The hills in the distance are still jagged but gray now. The dome overhead doesn't glitter, and the farm stretches to the edge. I'd love to use the nanos to figure out how far, but don't. My best guess is it's a few miles before the trees turn into shrubs and then into small plants.

As we get closer, I see how the first hundred rows or so of plants are small trees with thick leaves. They remind me of magnolias only the leaves are inky black instead of dark green. Turkh and G'nar might be able to see over them if they stand on tiptoes. There's no way I could. The work area here seems sunnier and less oppressive than the mines. I glance over at the men and spot G'nar tucking four of the bags into his beltline. Good idea and I do the same as does Turkh. "At least there are no bodies to put on the conveyor belt."

G'nar shakes his head "It's not easier up here. Debris is what they're calling the bodies."

Shit. I imagine the worst. The trees are poisonous and

the green goo they feed us is waste material. I want to ask if people drop like flies out here, only they'd give me that blank, "Must be an Earther thing," stare. Instead, I ask, "Are there a lot of deaths in the fields?"

"Only in the beginning. Once people realize the securbots mean business, they settle down."

Like the mine. Cool. I glance around. Current workers and new people are mixed together and are the only humanoids around. Securbots fly around like Earth's drones, pausing every so often before resuming. "Are they the eyes and ears of the ones in charge of this place?"

"In a way," Turkh answers. "They're automatic, checking for stationary people to threaten back into work. There's too many of us to watch individually, plus the ones running the place don't want to spend the salary on wages."

"I'd noticed there was only one guard today." A look passes between the two men as we continue on to non-occupied rows. "What do you suppose it means?"

"Could be anything. They could be closing shop, opening a new mine somewhere else, or just reassigned to a more problematic area." Turkh puts a hand on my shoulder, the first time he's touched me since we met up with G'nar. "Don't worry about it. Just refrain from using the nanos and keep your focus."

"We'll try to contact the Alliance," G'nar adds. "The main thing is to keep busy." He stops at the first of the unoccupied rows. "We can eat as much as we'd like, but it doesn't take a lot to fill you up. The main goal is getting the five bags full and dropped. The pick up process is automated and happens just before the sun has set for the day."

"You don't have two sets of people, one working while the other sleeps? And where do you go to sleep?"

"What about washing and waste?" Turkh adds from his row between G'nar and me.

He begins picking the fruit as he answers. "The stone pad just before we get bags is where we wash up. It's nice. The water sprays up from small holes and is warm, but I get cold afterward. I grab my bags and work until my clothes dry. I keep warming as the day goes on." He gives me a sly grin. "As for waste, look around. You go behind the nearest tree."

Both of them chuckle before a securbot buzzes up. I refocus on my job gathering fruit and ignore the machine. It moves on after a while. My shoulders are tight, and I turn my head side to side to loosen up. Somehow, working in the mine with Turkh felt more intimate than being out here with him. Maybe because now we are both on our best behavior around G'nar. They're up ahead of me a few feet already, and I try to pick up the pace. If it's like the mine out here, my keeping busy matters more than how fast I work. Which is great because if they're expecting me to be as good as two Alliance officers, I'm sunk.

Despite my best efforts, I fall behind as the day wears on. I taste test the fruit. The outer skin is bitter, but the meat inside is decent. They remind me of tasteless mangos with a much smaller pit. The dark leaves absorb the sunlight, and the warmth radiates to me. Eventually, I've filled one, then two, and finally three bags before Turkh is walking toward me.

"How are you doing?"

"It's going a lot slower than I'd planned."

"Sorry for leaving you behind. We're going to lag behind this afternoon so you can catch up."

"Don't get into trouble on my account."

He pulls his last bag from his beltline. "We won't. G'nar has filled me in on the expectations. As long as we're working and there's movement, they're forgiving of work speed." He picks and tosses fruit into his bag. "The work stops after sunset, and we sleep wherever we can find a place."

"Good to know." I watch for a few seconds as he works on my side of his row. I never thought to leave fruit on the opposite side of the trees. "Are you sure we can't use innercoms to talk?"

"Positive. Not up here where the signal could be clearer. Plus, we want to be ready for the Alliance's signal. Can't do that if we're chitchatting."

I keep working and hold my thoughts to myself. If Turkh had shown any of Rick's attitude, I'd be pissed over his "we" talk with G'nar being important while our "we" talk was chatter. "All right. Can I access internal databases?"

"Sure, I don't see why not. Just don't try to go beyond yourself for information. We'll be able to access the fabric soon enough once we leave here."

"Fabric?"

"Yeah, the blanket of waves our information system sends out."

"Ah." So, no web means there might not be spiders on Ghar. I'm sold on going there. "I promise, no trying to access beyond my own nanos."

"Good." He leans over and gives me a quick kiss. "I'm going on up to join G'nar. We're working on a second plan, so you're included when we leave."

All of my reservations evaporate as I realize neither man must let me tag along. "Thank you, Turkh. I promise I'll make sure letting me go with you two is worth the trouble."

"No need to thank a man for him keeping his mate." He gives me another quick kiss. "I'll be back later to check on you. If there are any emergencies, use the innercom."

"All right." Watching him walk away is both good and bad. Good, because that butt and those legs. Hell, the whole man is sex on a stick. Bad, because I miss him already. The guy is like an invasive ivy plant with tendrils all over my heart.

I shake my head and get back to work. Pick, drop, pick, drop, over and over until my third bag is full. There's a string tie, and I cinch it up. Another stubby tree, another space bag to fill. I take one of the juicier fruits and eat. The taste is still bland, and it helps my thirst. I wonder if the stuff they feed us is green from the additives because these are like giant grapes, pale on the inside.

The afternoon wears on, and I sneak away to pee

several rows away from mine. Before resuming work, I look up and down my row. Behind isn't very long while ahead stretches on until it disappears. I don't think I'll finish picking the entire row today. I work and concentrate on improving. I want a decent break time. With Turkh. Lots and lots of him.

I'm lost in daydreams about what he'd be like on Earth, what his homeworld must look like, how his family acts, and how grateful I am in him never meeting my mom.

Not until everything around me is glowing do I look up. The dome is glittering again as the sky is a deep blue. Azure clouds, thin and wispy, reflect teal light while puffier clouds reflect pinks and yellows. Different chemicals in the atmosphere must be sending back light along spectrums I've never seen on Earth. I smile. Turkh and I might be in serious trouble for the nanos I have, but I wouldn't change it. It's wonderful to know what I'm seeing when I look at the world now. Everything was such a blur before then.

I manage to stuff the last fruit into my final bag and tie it up. None of the prior four are behind me anymore. The pickup machines must be eerily quiet. The row doesn't end ahead of me, even if I'm done. The dark blue sky is nearly black as the sun sinks below the horizon. There's no light out here at all. I'm not afraid of the dark, but being alone in a field isn't the best, either.

"Lin? Are you done, yet?"

I can see Turkh ahead when he steps into my row, and I relax. "I am. Just now." There's just enough twilight left for me to catch a glint from his skin. Seriously, if he upped and told me he was an android, I'd totally believe him. He's too perfect to be a normal man, or alien.

"We're up a little way. Several others have gathered and are sharing stories."

I take his offered hand and let him lead me there. Being around others doesn't sound appealing. I'd enjoyed my alone time up here today since I never had peace and quiet while in the mine. I give Turkh's hand a squeeze. Plus, I'd like to find a place secluded with him.

"We'll stay for a little while, be social, and then find somewhere to sleep."

"With G'nar?"

"No. Nearby maybe, but far enough away for privacy."

"Even without innercom, you're reading my mind."

He turns me around and kisses me. "I'd like to read all of you, but later. We need to establish ourselves as part of the group in case we need their help."

"Are there problems?" I put my arms around him for the warmth and because he's so irresistible. His shirt is soft against my skin.

"Always, but none in particular. I just want to be ready with backup in case we need it. Fostering camaraderie will help."

"Then, let's be friendly," I say, and he silences me with a deeper kiss.

12

LIN

Dɪᴅ I sᴀʏ I ᴡᴀɴᴛᴇᴅ ᴛᴏ ʙᴇ sᴏᴄɪᴀʟ? Sɪᴛᴛɪɴɢ ᴀʀᴏᴜɴᴅ ᴀ bunch of bros, no matter what their color or fur, they're still bros, and listening to them one-upping each other is not my idea of an otherworldly good time. I could have stayed on Earth for this. Looking at you, Rick. Looking at you.

Anyway, after I shuffled over to Turkh's left side, his arm made the perfect leaning post. His race has dominant hands, too, and he tends to talk with his. I tried to listen to everything, but new muscles began aching. I didn't know some of them even existed. During a lull in the talking, I lean in and get his attention. "I'm about to fall asleep. Can you make sure no one follows me to bed?"

He moves to put an arm around me and draws me closer. "I'll do better and will follow you myself."

"You don't need to if you're having fun here."

He kisses the top of my head. "I need to let the others

get the message you're mine." After another kiss, he leans away, "Hey, my mate and I are going to sleep for the night. Thank you for the great company tonight."

He helps me to my feet as the others catcall. I can't help but blush. "We're not, I mean, not yet. Pre mates." Which doesn't help, judging by the increase in teasing. Turkh puts his arm around my shoulders, helping me ignore the embarrassment.

As we walk, he lets his hand slip down to hold mine as we walk. "Let's find a place to sleep under the stars and far from everyone else."

Focusing on other things, I think of our beds. "We don't have anything to sleep on except dirt and maybe leaves."

"You can sleep on me."

"I could, but then you'd be dirty."

He swoops me into his arms and lowers into a seated position. I'm on his lap as he growls, "I don't mind getting dirty for you."

His words go through me like a shot of adrenalin. I look toward the others, their voices faint in the darkening evening. "How alone are we?"

"Enough for this," he says before taking my lips in a kiss.

Finally. He's still cool to my touch, yet warmer than the surrounding area. I ease up without breaking our lip lock and straddle him. He rewards me with a mouth-tingling moan. I wrap my arms around his neck and wiggle my butt against his erection. He leans back to pull off his shirt, and it's my turn to moan. He's luscious. I put my hands on his chest as he lies down while holding me close. We bump noses and smile until he pulls my shirt off, too.

He looks at my breasts before glancing up at my face. I can barely see him in the low light, but the white of my bra sort of glows. "What is this? A secondary covering?

I smile because while I'd love to tell him it's an over the shoulder boulder holder, the explanation would take up too much of our sexy fun time. "Yes, a covering to keep tender parts safe." I peel off my bra and let it slide down. His gleeful surprise and reverence make me chuckle until he takes a nipple into his mouth. I want to cry out, but the others would hear. That's all I'd need. A bunch of alien men trying to rescue me from the sexiest guy I've ever seen. "Turkh?"

"Umm-hmm?"

"Can we do everything tonight?"

"Pless, I hope so." He stops licking my other nipple to look up and kiss me again.

His lips give me the shivers every time we touch. I can't help but run my hands over his smooth skin. I almost want to consult the datalinks on how to please a Gharian male, but then, finding out for myself sounds a lot more fun. I reach down between us, wanting to get a better idea of his size. I can't help but squeak out at his impressive size. Even through his pants, he's hot and hard. "Is this all for me?"

"Every bit."

"Good answer." I slip my hand into his waistband

and...jackpot. After running my hand down his length, I shiver. The man is ribbed for my pleasure. Not huge rings around his cock, but enough to feel when I stroke him. "Umm, are you a typical male?"

"Very, why?"

"No reason. I love typical." I resume kissing him while pulling his pants down and freeing his cock.

He breaks off my kiss to say, "Stand up."

"Hmm?" I ask before doing as he ordered. Turkh gets to his knees while holding me up. My legs are wobbly as he pulls my pajama bottoms and underwear down to my ankles. He hugs me close and buries his nose in my pubic hair. It's been a while since I've used anything resembling soap, so I try to turn away. "We might need to visit a bathing planet for that, Turkh."

He looks up at me and grips my butt cheeks. "What did you say about everything?"

"I..."

His quiet laugh interrupts me from giving an excuse. "Don't worry. Everything can be later after a long bath together." His hands circle my waist as he pulls me down towards him. "Right now, I want you, just you." Our hips align with his cock in between our stomachs as he says, "You're mine. I'm yours."

"Yes," I croak and slide down his shaft. "Are you ready?"

"Have been since we met." He lies back, holding me close until I slip my hands up to his chest.

I laugh and gasp when his cock head touches my

pussy. "All right." I ease down to envelop him. He lifts his hips up and grinds into me. His girth and length are size appropriate, and I love it. If we were anywhere near a more private place, I'd tell him just how good he feels. The slight ridges stuttering into me as he strokes me, his cock caressing my inner walls, his heat, and how good it is to be full of such a man wipes out anything I've ever experienced before now. As I bottom out, our pelvic bones as close as his length will allow, I bend down to rest my breasts against his pectoral muscles. "You feel so good," I pant in his ear as he thrusts up into me.

"Stop thinking, Lin. Let yourself feel," he replies in a whisper.

Before I can ask how, a rush of emotion and sensation flood my mind. His desire and erotic feelings are transmitting into my mind loud and clear. I don't pick up the physical touch he gets from me but am instead swamped in the pleasure our bodies together provide him. "Ohhh, we are good together, aren't we?"

"The best." His hands slide down my back to my butt, and he squeezes. "Fuck, you feel good. Better than I imagined."

My fingertips dig into his shoulders in glee over the thought of him fantasizing about me. I should reply, but he's so overwhelmingly good. I can't even think, never mind form words while he's moving inside me a little faster every few seconds.

"I'm close," he gasps in my ear. "I can't hold back."

An explosion of pleasure fills me as he climaxes. I feel

weak from the rush and more than a little shaky. His intense satisfaction almost makes up for my lack of one. "Wow!" I breathe, lying on his chest as he calms a little. "That was good. Thank you."

"You don't know about Gharian men, do you?" he asks, and I shake my head against his chest. "Then you don't know." He snorts a laugh. "I'm not done with you yet."

Turkh might want to do more, but it'll have to be later when he recovers. Still, I like his optimism. "Oh? Will we plan on this again tomorrow night?"

"Plan for right now." He lifts his hips and drives in a little deeper, his cock still hard and ready inside me. "We climax twice. Once to get the body ready, and again to complete the goal."

I move against him and place my hands on his shoulders. "So if I want to keep going, you'll let me until I come, too?"

"Sure, all night if you need to, as long as I get a few minutes of sleep before work tomorrow." He runs his hands up to my breasts and rubs my nipples with his thumbs. "You are so beautiful." He rises up enough to lick between my breasts before teasing my nipples with his tongue.

The tickle from his lips pulses to my core. Between the gentle rocking of his amazing body and the feel of his substantial length sliding deep into me, my climax hits hard. My toes clench, and I want to scream his name at the first few pulses. Instead, I keep quiet and send every ounce of pleasure to him via our link, and soon he comes a second time.

Sated, I relax against his chest. His heart beats under my ear and I smile as it slows in our afterglow. "If I didn't ache in places I never knew existed, I'd want to do this all over again."

"Tomorrow night for sure."

"Pless yeah." I smile when he laughs, and I add, "I know. Never in front of your family."

"Good. I want them to love my bonding mate as much as I do."

"Bond" and "mate" are binding words in most languages, including mine. The idea of being tied to this man for the rest of my life is both terrifying and exhilarating. "So, are we now in a union, or does there need to be a formal ceremony?"

"Yes, we're bonded. Anything more is something to make mothers and grannies happy while giving the bachelors a chance to seduce the bachelorettes."

"Funny how some things are the same no matter where you go." As our hearts slow, I rise up, trying to see him in the dark. "We ought to get dressed. I don't want someone to stumble across us in the morning."

"I agree." He sits up, taking me with him. "Since I have infrared vision, let me help you dress."

"How do you know I don't have the same ability?"

He pulls my shirt over my head. "You're from Earth. We're not born with the capability, either. Even my people need augmentation to see in the dark." He pulls up his pants and reaches forward to pull up mine, too. "Light pollution on Ghar is so prevalent, most of us don't get the additional functionality to our sight."

Now that I'm away from him, it's freakin' cold out here. I feel sorry for the others sleeping alone. When I shiver, Turkh leans forward and takes my thighs. "You can sleep on me tonight. Your pah jamahs won't keep you warm."

I laugh at his pronunciation and can't help but tease. "No 'h's' in pajamas, Turk-ha."

"Funny woman." He pulls me down on him as he lies back. Tucking one arm under his head while the other crosses over me, he adds, "With a smart tongue."

"It is. Just wait until you see what I can do with it after washing every inch of your body." I wiggle my hips for emphasis.

He runs a hand down his face before letting the palm rest on my upper back. "The Alliance needs to come get us soon."

I smile as his protectiveness puts me to sleep. The next thing I know, distant voices wake me. Thankfully, I didn't drool on him in my sleep. When I look up, I see he's already conscious and staring up at the sky. The light peeking in among the trees seems warmer than last night's sunset. The early morning rays give Turkh's facial hair a bit of a glint. I want him all over again. In fact, I want more everything. More information, more variety of foods, and especially more alone time with him. He's a handsome man, inside and out, and if I had to travel light years to find him? I'm okay with that. "Good morning."

He looks down his chest at me with a smile. "Good morning. How are you feeling?"

My toes wiggle when I think about last night, and I can't help but return his grin. "Sore in all the right places and wanting a planet to ourselves. But I'd settle for a repeat performance tonight if you're willing."

Turkh chuckles before frowning. I lift up my head and shoulders. "Everything all right?"

"Yeah. G'nar is awake and says the Alliance is trying to contact him. He wants me to be ready for the signal."

"How do you do that?" I scramble to settle in beside him as he sits up. "Is it difficult or will it hurt you?"

"Neither." He puts an arm around me. "It's more like I need to open my mind to their frequency and wait for the databurst."

"Sounds easy enough."

"The transmission block by the Vahdmoshi makes receiving anything a challenge." He stands and brushes the dirt from his behind and the back of his head.

I stand, too, and sweep his back. His yummy muscles might have me lingering a little too much. "I suppose instead of pestering you with questions, I could be asking the nanos everything." As soon as I say the words, a channel in my mind is opened. It's like a webpage on a computer at home. Pictures flash too fast for me to really look at them. They crowd in, rapid-fire, overwhelming me.

I'm frozen in place but manage to squeak out, "Turkh? Something's happening."

I feel him whirl around against my touch more than see him. My vision is too crowded, and my stinging pain begins.

"Lin! Block the signal. Turn off access."

He shakes me, but I can't move. "I can't..." I croak before the entire universe shuts down.

13

TURKH

I catch Lin before she crumples to the ground, and sink to my knees, letting the loose soil cushion us both. Any Gharian civilian accepting a military databurst would have trouble with the speed, but a newly upgraded Earther? I can't imagine the pain and confusion in her mind right now. Or what would be there if she were conscious. "Lin? Sweetheart, if you can hear me, you need to block access to everyone and everything." I smooth hair from her forehead. "Please, Lin, wake up and tell me you're all right."

No answer. I try reaching out to her mentally and emotionally, but she's quiet. Alive, but silent. There's a rustle in the trees. I look over as G'nar approaches. He probably can guess, but I tell him, "She took the databurst meant for us."

"Pless." He comes up and kneels beside her. "Can you access her programming remotely?"

"I haven't tried yet. She just passed out." I pull her closer, letting her head rest against my chest. "Come on, Lindsey, wake up for us."

"I've been talking with the others. The systems watch the fields for movement and resting heart rate from the translators. They're going to know when she's unconscious and send a bot after her." He kneels down next to me. "Take her to the end of the row. They haven't set up sensors up there, yet, and you should be safe until she's awake."

I nod because I don't trust my voice enough to speak. Instead, I get to my feet, still cradling her in my arms. After clearing my throat, I tell G'nar, "I'll go to the end, if possible. Could you grab enough bags for the three of us in case she recovers before then?" He gives me a nod and goes toward the opposite end of the rows.

I kiss Lin's forehead and take off toward the farthest part of the vast farm. While in motion, I reach out with my sensors to detect how strong the Vahdmoshi signal to the translators is. She's still out, and I kiss her face. "Come on, dearest, wake up for me." I keep my lips against her skin and reach into her programming.

She's shut down completely. I feel her heartbeat and breathing. The signal barely reaches me, yet I don't want to relax here. An Alliance message precursor tingles at the edge of my mind, and I know they've sensed something wrong. I need to get Lin to safety and take the time to explain to my director what's happening down here.

As I hurry down the row with her, the trees turn into

shrubs before shrinking to freshly planted sprouts. I don't like how we're open prey for the securbots, but the rocks up ahead look somewhat sheltering. It's as if giants shoved everything aside to create flat and level fields. The boulders are probably leftovers from mining proth as much as machines could accomplish. I slink between two huge mountains of rock with a space barely wide enough for me and Lin walk into. I don't like how hard the ground is here compared to in the fields, but it'll have to do until she wakes up enough to walk.

When I'm sure the broadcast is faint, I settle in to sit and keep her steady in my arms. I lean back and can relax a little to focus on her. She's still out, but her eyelids are fluttering. I give her a squeeze. The processing after a databurst is draining. *G'nar? Grab some fruit on your way here?*

Will do.

He sends his plans and a rough sketch of the surroundings. The securbots can shoot this far but aren't programmed to go this beyond a small radius to their docking area. We're lucky they're using the lower quality on the planet. The latest and greatest could reach more places than anything on two or four feet.

A moan from Lin stops everything. I stare down at her face. "Lin? Honey?"

"Turkh?" She shakes her head, her eyes squeezed shut. "What the hell? Have I been hacked? Can nanos be turned against me?

"No, you'll be fine." I brush hair against her temple

and kiss. I'd do anything to take on her pain as my own. "You received a message meant for G'nar or me."

"Oh, good." Her eyes flicker open, and I've never been happier to see blue in my life. "I'd hate for you guys to go through this."

"We do it all the time." I hold her close and can feel her smile against my chest. "Our systems are equipped for it. Yours isn't."

"Was it a mistake? Should I send everything to you and G'nar?"

Her sweet voice is tired. My poor love. "Mistake for it to be sent to you, yes. We'll be sure to receive the information directly the next time a window opens."

Are you behind the slurry?

Yes, we both reply at once. Lin leans back and grins at me. "Sorry. I heard him, too."

"He'll be here in a few seconds," I say before kissing her. She feels better than I remember and I love how her tongue licks my lips. I pull away first and say to her slight protest, "Later, I promise."

She grins, but before she can say anything, G'nar turns the corner. "Good move to hide here." He approaches with a quarter bag full of fruit. "Here's breakfast and maybe lunch if she needs more time."

Lin sits up and reaches for the food. "Thank you. I'm starving all of a sudden."

As she bites into a fruit, I look at G'nar. "How much trouble do you think we're in?"

"You know as well as I do." He rubs between his eyes.

"Problem is, if we don't get the signal, send back our evidence, and get out of here clean, nothing we feel for her will matter."

"We?" Lin says and looks from me to him. "Don't tell me you've gone soft for a mangy Earther like me."

G'nar snorts and hands me a fruit then takes one for himself. "If all Earth women are like you, I might end up not resenting the trouble you're going to cause me." He looks up. "Anyway, the Alliance should be trying again any seco—"

"Identify yourself," rings out in my mind. The three of us look at each other for confirmation the others heard, too.

Lin's eyes are large in her face as she gets to her feet. "What do I say?"

I shake my head and stand, too. "Deny them access, Lin. Block all incoming messages."

A flash of pain fills her expression. "Even yours?"

KirKrell Turkh, identify unknown receiver near you. G'nar, identify unknown receiver near you. Pless it all. They're not going to be happy with a simple, "There's no Earther here," from either of us. "Especially block me. G'nar too."

G'nar gives me my bag quota and gives Lin hers. "I'll ask for the data, send it to you when they're done. In the meantime, remove her bionans."

"No." Lin stumbles while backing away from me. "I'm not giving them up to you or anyone else."

I glance at G'nar. He's right. It would be better if I stripped the foreign tech from her before another

151

databurst. One received by an unknown is an anomaly. Two received is our butts in a vise. Plus, I need more time to run simulations on the three of us getting out of here. I try to smile and focus on Lin. "Come on. I'll be quick, and the removal won't be permanent."

Except, if we're sent to an eighth world, it will be permanent. I can't hide this from her but try to anyway. "I'll do what I can to give you civilian nanos when we're on Ghar. Just let me deactivate everything I've sent to you before the Alliance gets here."

She stares at both of us before shaking her head. "You're lying to me. All of that chatter about bonding and our union and my being your mate was what? A way to keep the Earther calm and her legs spread?"

Pless, Turkh. You didn't have to go that far to placate her.

"Both of you know I didn't lie about anything." I turn to Lin. "Look, you're picking up on deception from me because I don't know what will happen once the Alliance finds out we're mated. I just don't want them to blame you for my giving you tech beyond your capabilities. That's it. I'm being as honest as I can with what information I have."

G'nar standing behind me must be backing my truth because her frown softens by the time she looks from him to me. She nods. "All right, but I'm not giving these up for anyone or anything. Not until I'm safely off of here." She takes a few steps back, one hand holding a half-eaten fruit, the other up as if to ward us away. "I've done as you suggested and tried to not use them, especially not to communicate. But I don't want to shut them down completely."

"It's not a question of what you want, Lin."

I turn to G'nar and think *Shut it.* "Don't. I'm taking care of the problem." As soon as I refocus on Lin, her face is whiter than a Blendarian's underbelly. "What's wrong?"

"You're taking care of a problem?" She puts a hand to her head. "I can't even think right now, yet you're calling me a 'problem.' Is a bondmate a 'problem' to you?"

"No, of course not." I know she's half delirious with pain, but I'm desperate to calm her. "You're my love, but we have to be smart about this. I can't present an Earther with bionans to the Alliance. They'll exile both of us and probably not together."

She glances at G'nar before stepping back again. "No. You're not taking my only means of communication with authorities. I don't care who's in charge. I want a way to get information."

I don't look at G'nar as he snorts before he says, "Stop being a child. Bionans are just a new toy for you to play with and now it's time for you put them away." *Turkh, do I need to hold her down while you extract them, or are you able to?*

Fleegan! I send to him as Lin bolts. She's running deeper into the mounds of discarded ore, toward the end of the dome.

G'nar gets in my face and pokes a finger in my chest. "Don't you call me a fleegan. You both know what to do about Alliance tech. We don't have a lot of time before the

Alliance comes in and closes us down. Do you want to be responsible for the slaughter of the lesser worlders here? I know you care for Lin, but are you willing to pay for her with the lives of all the others?"

I can't answer him because I know what I should say. Yet, I love her. There has to be a way to accomplish the mission and be with Lin at the same time. Projecting a confidence, I don't quite feel, I say, "We're saving the lesser and completing our mission, then. Go blend in with the farmers while I bring back Lin."

"Her bionans?"

"I'll strip as many as I can."

I turn to leave as he says, "Wait. I'm not trying to be a fleegan about this. You've always known it's mission first. You took the oath, too."

"I know. Let me do my job." I turn and head off in Lin's direction. She might have the schematic to the dome's layout via the databurst. I try to tap into her bionans, but she's blocked me. *Lin, come on. We need to talk.*

Silence.

Damn. I really don't like intruding. *Lin, I have a military override for civilians in danger. It's mentally invasive, and I don't want to use it.*

So don't.

Even though I want to, I don't smile at how easy it is to pick up her location. *Lin, please. We need to go back to the main area and wait for word from our director. I need the databurst from you, and you need to stop using the nanos.* I can also tell from infrared she's been through here. Before

I'm able to say anything else, an alarm sounds in the distance. The crude translator in the back of my neck begins to ache.

Turkh?

They know we're away from our post. I switch gears. *G'nar?*

We're done. *They know about the three of us and will raze the planet to rubble if you don't come back.*

Lin, did you get that?

I did. She steps out from around a large mound. "I'll go back with you. Just don't touch me. Under any circumstances, got it?"

Now that she's forbidden me, all I want to do is hug her until she trusts me again. I shake my head. "I won't touch you."

She glares at me. "Not even if I'm about to die from a brain aneurysm. Which honestly feels like any minute now."

Enduring the databurst's effects on her were bad enough. There is no way in the universe I could stand by and watch the life slip from her body. I couldn't bear her death. "No, I can't promise that."

She crosses her arms, still holding those damned gathering bags. "Then I stay here and let them gun me down."

The mental image of her dying terrifies me. "No. You'll do no such thing." I rush up to her. "Do not make me drag you there just to keep you alive."

Lin holds up her hands and takes a few stumbling

steps backward. "I won't if you promise not to remove the nanos until I'm ready."

"Fine." She's killing me. She knows what promises mean in my culture. "I promise to not touch you even if doing so saves your life."

"Thank you. I'm not sure I can trust you, but thank you." She begins walking toward me, and a stun beam hits her chest. She falls to the ground and whatever I said a few seconds ago is gone as I dive to her.

"Lin!" I begin crawling to her limp body, but before I can reach her, another stun beam hits my back. Everything overloads as the pain smothers me.

"Did you know they were Alliance?"

I don't recognize the voice. The ground is cold and smooth under me, not the cold and rough of what seemed a few seconds ago. I reach out for Lin and G'nar on the innercom but can't ping them. I pray to Origin that they're merely unconscious.

"No. None of us guessed they were anything but chattel. No one's ever sent us anything but sixth and seventh worlders."

Two are in here at least. One's the boss, another's getting raked. If there are any others, they're letting someone be their spokesman. I want to peek but don't want to tip them off about my regaining consciousness.

"So you never think, hey, those two look like Gharians. Maybe we should scan them and see if they are?"

Turning on emotional dampeners because yeah, this observation is amusing. It's also something we'd counted on when landing and blending into the crowd.

"No. We didn't."

"I see. One of them is already awake. Wake up the other two so we can talk."

Pless it. At least now I know the other two are here and all right. There's no need in playing durika, so I lift up my head before sitting. "I'll do it. I'll wake them both."

"See? I told you one of them was awake." The man talking looks like a Vahdmoshi but with a thin, wide mouth and big beady eyes. His daddy was from Gleet, or more probably his mom was. I try not to smirk at the insult. My back aches as I get to my feet and he motions with a webbed hand. "Get going, then. And you." He turns to the other guard. "I want everyone on your team in here now."

"Yes, sir."

He scrambles as I look behind me. Lin and G'nar are there, tossed together like limp rags. I want to pull them apart. She's mine. I'm hers. I take a deep breath to calm the jealousy surging through me.

"Why are they not awake yet, Gharian?"

The raspy voice of the Vahd leader sets my irritation on edge. I turn to the two where they lie. "Give me a few moments. They're out cold."

"You have until the guards are here."

Resisting the urge to smart off to him, I go to Lin's side first and kneel. "Lin, dearest." I pick her up from G'nar,

157

and he stirs. "Come on, buddy, let's wake up." G'nar opens an eye. "Yes, you. They want us coherent for our deaths."

"Pless," he mutters and gets to his elbows.

"I know." Lin is still limp, and I try to access her programming via the innercom. *Bondmate, time to wake up.* I pull her to me. *We need to be alert for this.*

No. Go away. I'm so tired and don't like you at all.

I can't help but chuckle at her rebellious tone. *I am, too, but wake up for me and I'll leave a lot sooner.* Her eyes open and I smile. "Good. Let's wake all the way up." Three guards and their leader shuffle in, cutting off what I was going to say next.

"All right." The mixed species leader gets to his feet. "Who of you knew we had an Earther and two Gharians among the workers?"

The men look at each other like guilty schoolchildren. None of them want to admit to fucking up, of course.

"None of you noticed? Really?" He comes out from around his desk with his hands clasped behind him. "You're telling me in a mix of Gleetars, Blendarians, MoNsi, and Mrwars with a few Khsccs thrown in because Khscc was on the way, these three didn't stand out to any of you?"

He walks in front of each man, and I'm glad we're not them. The guards scuff their feet and give furtive looks to one another as Lin sits up. I ease back to provide her with more space as G'nar pushes himself up, too. *We may have to run,* he sends me, and I glance at Lin. She gives me a slight nod.

"We're understaffed, sir. I figured a few errors wouldn't matter." The lead guard shrugs and looks to the others for support. "I mean, it's not like we meant to get an Earther in the mix."

"Oh." The leader lets go of his hands and lifts them high before letting them down with a plop on his belly. "I feel so much better. You didn't mean to break Alliance law."

I frown at G'nar. *Law? Isn't this whole setup illegal?* G'nar shrugs. I clear my throat, wanting to give him something else incriminating to rant about while we record everything, and say, "Why just one Earther, too? I mean, we could have been picked up accidentally while slumming it with one of those Khscc women or sneaking out of Mumbani's salacious zones, but the Earther? How does *that* happen and why stop at one?"

He nods. "Good point, Gharian." After walking up to his chief guard, he adds, "Well? Tell me we didn't waste fuel going for one tiny Earther so you could all gawk at the forbidden."

"We stopped for more than her, sir. There were several, eight or nine. Most died on the way here while three more died in the mines and one was killed in the fields." He goes over to Lin and points at her sleeve. "Even she was hit during an altercation. I figured she was dead as well or I'd have told you about her." He lifts his chin. "Taking on Earthers was a trial. If it had been successful, we would gain nearly eight billion new workers. It didn't, so we're stuck with the usual thirty billion to draw from."

Doesn't seem like a lot of people for a galaxy's population.

I don't smile at Lin's observation. *He's counting the fifth to seventh worlds. Second to fourth have forty billion combined.*

And the first worlds?

We don't know. They won't allow us to access their tech.

Smart of them to not let inferior beings access anything of theirs.

I look down to keep from smiling at her barb. By now, the planet's leader is seated at his desk, the interrogation paused. He's quiet for a moment before finally speaking. "I have a mess now, thanks to you, all of you, who didn't pull these three from the workers and tell me about them. Instead, I'm sure the Alliance is on its way to rescue their two Protectors and their Earth pet.

Before I can correct him about Lin's status, G'nar steps forward. "We're Enforcers, not Protectors."

"Oh. Impressive." He stands. "Well, then, guards. You're done. You've really put the operation into jeopardy. We will need to dismantle the entire operation before the Alliance does it for us." After pressing a button on the desk surface, four men in red uniforms step in. "The guards need to be executed and the Gharians released outside of the dome."

The guards' leader steps forward to speak but is shot by the red security detail. The sudden action startles Lin, and I pull her closer. I want to ask about his plans for her, but the detail kills the remaining guards.

G'nar glances at me and addresses the leader. "You're releasing all of us to die outside? Why?"

"Not all three of you. You and your Gharian brother there will accidentally die from the lack of air. I certainly didn't have any second world Protec—I mean, Enforcer executed." He shrugs. "If anyone asks, you two made a run for it and died in the attempt."

We need a plan for staying together, so I ask, "What about her? Is she going back to work or being let out with us?"

"Her kind are useless in our mines. Too weak." He waves over a red guard. "Plus, her planet won't retaliate in any meaningful way, so I see no reason to keep her alive."

14

LIN

Turkh steps in front of me. I can't let him be killed. "You can't kill me," I say, trying to stall for time while searching the bionan database for something legal to scare him with. "Because..." At last, the knowledge drops and now I have an argument. "Because I'm now a second world citizen. If you kill me outright, you'll hang."

"Hang?"

"Hang in this context is an Earth colloquialism meaning corporal punishment," I say as if I'm a computer. "You are already in serious legal trouble by kidnapping me and the others from Earth. Their deaths can be explained as accidents if any proof can be found. Killing me, though?" I step out from behind Turkh. "There are too many witnesses. You should send me out with the men and let me die accidentally." I use air quotes around "accidentally," and no, I'm not proud of myself. But really, we all knew the word needed the quotes when he said it first.

"Fine. I don't care either way." He sighs. "Which one of you is her bondmate?"

"I am," Turkh answers.

He peers hard at G'nar before turning to the red guards. "Take all three to the exit. Shoot to kill if they try to escape before then."

I look to Turkh first then G'nar to join in any protest they make, but they're silent. They have a plan, I hope, and one that includes me. The red guards approach us, weapons drawn.

"This way."

We turn and follow the two guards out of the room. Now that I'm conscious, I look around for ways to escape or weapons to use. Nothing. The walls are a bare gray and look like they've been made out of concrete. Our footsteps echo in the emptiness. Or theirs do because I'm still shoeless. A securbot occasionally whirrs by us. They're like wasps and give me the chills despite the seemingly routine nature of their actions.

Lin?

I love Turkh's voice in my mind. He's not on my good side just yet but isn't on my bad, either. *Yes?*

You have emotional dampeners. Could you please use them while we talk?

I stop just short of nodding. Instead, I do as Turkh's asked and turn on the dampeners. *There. What's the plan?*

We don't have a lot of time, thinks G'nar to us. *There*

are two options. Talk the guards into letting us go or scatter and pick them off one by one. Then one of us would turn off the planetary signal block so we could get a message to the director.

Turkh sends me blueprints to the station. I don't smile even though I want to. *Where was this yesterday or the day before?*

Need-to-know basis, G'nar replies. *We don't have much farther before the main airlock. Lin, do you have any fighting skills?*

Not against armed assailants. Sorry I'm dead weight.

Can't be helped. In fact, start limping to draw their attention. Turkh and I will do the rest.

I glance at Turkh, and he gives me a slight nod. A few steps later, I stumble. "Ow!" I go to my knees and grab my ankle before falling to my butt. "It hurts! I've hurt my leg."

The guards circle me as the leader says, "Come on, nothing happened."

"Yes, it did." I'm rocking back and forth as if the pain is too much to bear. "I ran into one of these goons and stubbed my toe."

"Your toe," he says.

Maybe I should have tried out for a school play or taken drama because he doesn't seem to buy it. "Yeah, my toe. I stumbled and hurt it."

"Uh huh."

I bow down over my ankle. "I can't walk. It hurts too much."

"Pless, kill her and let's go."

A guard lifts his weapon to me as another says, "Not here. I'm on floor duty around here since Zars left. I'm not mopping up her diseased Earth blood."

"So don't. Let the leader see your laziness and your corpse can be next to hers."

"I am not la—"

G'nar slams into the lazy guard while Turkh rams into his buddy like rugby players. I scoot out of the way as the men shove the guards into each other. A gun falls and goes off. I crawl over and grab it, aiming at the tumbling and fighting bodies.

Squeezing the trigger does nothing. I smash it a few more times and nothing. I don't see a button or a safety. The bionans tell me it's DNA coded. "Damn it." I don't throw away the gun but keep it. Turkh and G'nar have the men piled up into a heap anyway.

"Good." G'nar gives me a genuine smile, the first I've seen, and he's actually rather gorgeous. Not Turkh gorgeous but still decent. He's also still talking. The bionans have a handy review function and I back it up.

He's said, "Let's grab everything. Can't use them, but if we have the weapons, they can't either."

Turkh and I follow G'nar's lead and grab up everything. One guard stirs, and Turkh punches him across the jaw again. "Stay down," he growls before pulling the gun from the man's limp hands.

The whirring sound of a securbot echoes against the bare walls. *Run!* flashes in my mind along with a map.

Turkh grabs my free hand, and we go up the hall and down a smaller corridor. The lighting is low, and after we pass a light fixture, the familiar securbot sound begins. Turkh looks at the bot before checking down the hall. "Stay with me."

He grabs my hand, and I drop the gun as he zigzags us down the corridor. The bot follows while spitting lasers at us. Turkh's movements are random enough for me to have a tough time keeping up. As soon as he finds the door, he gives it a couple of hard kicks. The securbot gets in a couple more shots. One rips into my right side, going through my waist. The emotional dampeners keep me from screaming as we fall inside.

I can't breathe from the pain. This makes what happened to my arm seem like a scratch and the databurst a sprained wrist. The room's automatic lights come on. Turkh's talking to me via the innercom. I pick out words like *block, safe,* and *temporary,* but my injury overpowers everything.

"Are you all right?"

He's next to me, and his spoken words break through my haze. I'm not sure how I found a box to sit on, but I'm here, and he's kneeling next to me.

"The bot hit you, didn't it?" He puts a hand on my knee. "Let me see how bad it is."

"All right. You look for us both." I turn my right side toward him while watching his face. He pales under his metallic skin. Now I know how badly I'm hurt. The bionans sent me messages, but I refused to listen. It's bad, and I can see the warning in my internal display outlined with red. Pushing off the freakout about dying until later, I take his face in my hands and look him in the eyes. "You need to go. Find another way out of here and link up with G'nar. The mission, remember?"

"No." He kisses my palm. "Let me stay here with you and talk with him first."

He's probably right. The securbot could still be out there or worse, calling for friends to help him blast into here. Unless... I put a hand on Turkh's arm. "The translators. They can track the three of us with them."

"They're nonfunctioning."

"Are you sure? Mine is giving me tingles, still."

"Let me see." He pulls my hair up from my neck and puts his fingertips over it. The sensation tickles for a moment before he lets my hair down and shows me the crude translator. "You might be a little sore there for a while. The bionans are busy elsewhere."

"And yours?"

He reaches back and retrieves his, too. "I don't feel a signal from them, but who knows? The Vahdmoshi had this place hidden for quite some time before we found it."

The room spins a little, and I hold on to the seat's edges for stability. "I might sit on the floor and lean against the box for support."

Turkh stands and crunches our devices under his heel. "I need to finish my message to G'nar. He's behind cargo in the ship hangar."

"He needs to remove his translator. Too bad we can't blow up the cargo without killing ourselves at the same time."

"Too volatile." His face goes blank, and I know he's talking with G'nar. I ease down to the floor. The pain radiates from my side through my arm and up my neck to cover half of my face. My body and the bionans want me to lie down and rest, but I'm afraid I won't wake up again. I want to be conscious until Turkh leaves. He glances at me while he's communicating. I can see the fear clearly on his face. I need to give up and die. Let him escape here in one piece.

My eyelids flutter closed until he begins shaking me. "Damn it, Lin, don't you dare. Stay with me." He's kneeling in front of me and places a knee on either side of my thighs where I sit. "We have one more thing to try. Understand?"

Everything is too difficult to do. I can't nod or even open my eyes. I try to send him a message mentally but am so tired. My chin falls to my chest as he says, "Dearest? Lin?" His hands tremble as he takes my face. "I swear I'm not being forward. You need everything I can give you."

He tilts my face up with a hand under each of my ears and kisses me. A deep, longing kiss and I feel the fear and concern in his touch. He licks my lips before running the tip of his tongue along my front teeth. I open for him, and the rush of endorphins feels almost as good as his caresses. "This has to work," he says against my mouth.

I try to smile and reassure him. The pain is already

fading to a numbness like I've drunk everything in my mom's liquor cabinet. "It'll be fine, I promise," I manage to whisper before the galaxy dims to black.

15

TURKH

I catch Lin before she falls back against the storage box. Pless it all to Tunsa, this is getting old. I should have just given her everything I had in the beginning when I knew what she'd be to me. My body is running a skeleton crew, and if I'd been smart at the start, I'd have had time to regenerate more bionans.

I settle in against the heavy boxes to make both of us more comfortable. We're together, and that is good enough for now.

How is she?

I have to be vague with G'nar about what I did. *She'll live.*

You didn't give more bionans to her, did you?

I had to. G'nar doesn't respond to my reply for a while. I reach out and add, *I couldn't sit here and watch her die.*

You two will be exiled and probably not together.

171

I can't argue because we both know the rules. *Let me send you a databurst from my experiences for the director.*

Good. I'm close to the blocker. I'll take it out, send our data, and wait for retrieval.

Stand by for transmission. I send my information from the time we landed until now, personal moments excluded.

Received. Taking blocker offline now.

An explosion rocks the building, shaking us both. *Was that you?*

Yes. Overdid it with the proth. Sending to Alliance now.

Stupidly, I nod as if he's here. Even if our director and his group don't pick up the signal right away, they will eventually, and the Vahdmoshi will be brought to justice. I give Lin a slight squeeze. "Just hold on and let the bionans do the work."

Turkh? Message sent. Pickup point in central cargo bay. Is she better?

Not yet.

Send me where you are. We can add my bionans to yours.

I think of how I added mine to Lin's body and a flare of jealousy burns in my chest. After glancing down at her, I realize my emotions are petty and useless if she dies. *Certainly. If she's not awake by the time you get here, let's do it.*

I can feel his slight laugh, and I know he's figured out my reluctance for the transfer to her. She's mine. I'm hers. Nothing anyone else does can break our union. I kiss the top of her forehead. The litany reminds me of what's essential and what isn't.

Every minute we've been together, she's amazed me. Her laugh despite the unforgiving surroundings. The way she smiles at me. How tough she's been through the harsh work we've been given. Everything she is makes me love her more with every passing minute. I stare down at her beautiful face. The side of her face where the proth hit her is a little red but not instantly noticeable. The rest of her skin is a bit dirty, yet pale and smooth. She'd be horrified if I admitted to knowing how she could use a bath. Anyone else would smell, well, a little too ripe. But her? I put my nose in her hair and breathe deep. I love her unique smell. It intoxicates me like nothing else can.

Lin can't die. If she does, then my soul dies, too.

The door's handle jiggles a little, and I think, *G'nar?*

He steps in, saying, "Yeah?"

"Glad it's you."

"Me too. Has she tried to regain consciousness?"

"Not yet, but then I haven't pushed her."

"Let me try." He sits down and leans forward, closer to her face. "Lin, honey, if you don't wake up, I'll have to give you a big, sloppy kiss."

"You're not," I growl.

"Oh yes, I am. If I don't, she might never wake up, and we'll be stuck on this plessed rock. So, I think it's worth it, even if I have to kiss a disgusting little Earther like her." He leans closer. "Maybe she wants my kiss. Maybe she likes all Gharian men."

Her nose wrinkles and she shakes her head a little. "Eh eh."

G'nar chuckles and glances at me. "You'll have to do better than that."

Like a child not wanting to face the day, she rolls over, and her nose touches my chest. I give a glare to G'nar in case he thinks of getting closer to us both. "Dearest, if you wake up now, we can leave here and ditch G'nar along the way. Sound good.?"

"Yeah." She puts a hand on my chest. "I'm trying. It's so hard 'cause I'm tired."

G'nar eases away from us and stands up. "Start moving now, and you'll become more alert." He claps his hands. "Come on, let's go, so I don't have to kiss you and get a beating from Turkh."

She sighs before struggling to sit upright on my lap. "All right. We've probably been here too long as it is."

"Did you cut the securbots?" I ask.

"For now." G'nar opened the door and looked both ways. "Once the lead guy discovers what I've done, it's going to be ugly and shoot to kill." He steps out of the room and makes a come-on motion.

We follow him out. Lin holds on to me while asking, "Do we have a plan?"

"We do," G'nar says. "The Alliance has the evidence, and we need to meet them at the pickup point."

"How far away is it?" I ask aloud but think him a message. *She's weak. The bionans don't have a lot of extra building material to work with.*

There's a mess hall of sorts. G'nar sends the location to me. *It's small, but there should be something for her to eat.* He gives Lin a brief smile. "We won't need to go far. Right now, we need to get you some food for the nanos to fix the gaping hole in your waist."

She tries to close the burn in her shirt as if doing so will hide the wound. "Sorry to be such a problem. I'm jeopardizing the mission, and Turkh should have left me in the fields until all of this was over."

"Yeah, we'd leave you just like you'd leave one of us," he says.

Lin glances at me, and I add, "We're all a team now. Get used to it." I detect a whirring noise and hold up a hand. *Hear that?* I send out to both of them. *The securbots are online again.*

Pless, we don't have long now.

No matter what else happens, we know the Vahdmoshi won't risk their dug up proth. If they shoot and miss us? Everything would be gone. I tilt my head. *Let's get to the mess hall, grab some food, and find our way to the cargo bay for pickup.*

We could skip eating. I'm not that hungry, Lin offers.

Neither G'nar nor I acknowledge her. She doesn't know how much she needs the nourishment for repairs. I take her hand, and we follow G'nar down the empty corridors to the mess hall. Or, as he opens the door, the tiny room of a mess hall. The three of us duck inside as a securbot goes by.

"This looks like a fridge." Lin heads for the cooling

unit and opens the door. "I suppose some things are the same everywhere." She begins going through the contents, reading the sides of containers and cartons.

I go to the doorway to keep watch for stray bots or angry guards. Lin's saying something to G'nar before he opens a can of juice for her. I try to stay focused on what's happening outside. Her face as she drinks Arnsa lite is adorable. The sour brew is an acquired taste. Soon, she's gulping the stuff down like a kid. G'nar's peeled a couple of rills for her. The rinds come off easily. He gives a leftover one to me. "Thanks. How soon can we make a break for it?"

"Whenever we're done." He bites into the fruit. I do the same, enjoying the best non-goo I've eaten since landing here. Ripeness matters. Who knew? "They have a huge mess to clean up in the control room first."

I can't help but grin. If there's anything G'nar knows how to do better than any other Alliance Enforcer, it's making a mess. I finish my last bite while checking to see if Lin's good. She gives me a slight smile. I'd take more for her to eat on the way, storing them in my pockets, but rill doesn't travel well. "Want more before we leave?"

"Maybe a few more drinks." She hurries to the food cooler and grabs another bottle of Arnsa lite, opening it with a twist.

"Bring it. You can toss the bottle anywhere when you're done."

G'nar steps past me to leave the room as I hold out my

hand for Lin. "He's right. Littering won't matter in another hour or two."

"Is that how long it'll take for the Alliance to get here?"

She's whispering, but it's not quiet enough. I reply, *Yes. Once they received the data, they knew to be on their way.*

We creep down the hallway with Lin between us. G'nar's first, peering around corners before we follow him. I hear a securbot's whine as it approaches, but the machine is flying fast. By the time I'm in front of Lin to protect her, it's already gone. The noise fades as I say, "That's not supposed to happen."

Lin nods and looks from me to G'nar before easing down to set the empty bottle on the floor. *I've seen them move like that on the way to kill troublemakers.*

G'nar gives us a slight grin. *Yet they didn't stop at us. Odd.*

I grin, too. We're lucky the bots are preoccupied, but it worries me. They're focused and I hope to Tunsa it's not what I think it is. Lin's hand slips into mine, and I give her a reassuring squeeze. Her coloring is returning to normal with every minute. We just need to get her off of this cursed rock and into second world care.

By the time two more securbots fly by us, we're dangerously used to their presence. I send a thought to both G'nar and Lin. *We need to worry more about the bots.*

I'm not bothered at all, Lin thinks to us. *I'll just pull you two in front of me this time.*

Ha. Ha. I don't have a death wish, G'nar replies.

I look ahead at the cargo bay doors. *We're close and no guards anywhere.*

I'm keeping them busy with a fire in the control room.

Nice. I feel a bit of guilt for how much he accomplished while I was busy with Lin. He is too distracted to say so now, but we both know she's worth the delay.

We stare out of the huge windows lining the other side of the hall. Each of us has a perfect view of the mine's opening and the fields beyond. We slide along the wall toward the cargo bay doors. A line of securbots fly toward both work areas, side by side. Various people stop and look up as the bots open fire.

"They're liquidating." I grab Lin's hand. "Fuck what our director wants. We need to leave now."

16

TURKH

My internal display lights up directions for me along the floor and walls as I lead Lin and G'nar to the cargo hangar. The automatic door is open. Shouting and jet blasts echo out as we hurry inside. No one notices us at first. They're all too busy making sure the delivery ships are able to take off for a safer place.

There's no roof other than the dome high above. Lin squeezes my hand, and I look down to see a guard pointing a gun at us. He takes a step forward, his eye up to the sight. "I should save time and just kill you all now."

G'nar glances up at the dome. "Or you could run for cover because the Alliance is almost here.

The guard looks up as shards of the canopy fly everywhere. One of the escaping ships is hit, almost cut in two, and the pieces go in different directions. Lin's gaze follows the smoking parts down while I look for shelter. If the Alliance follows procedures, every ship in the area will be scrap in an hour or so. The broken-up craft falls into the fields, exploding on impact. The guard holsters his gun. "I'm out. You're on your own." He takes off for one of the cargo ships as its engines begin to fire.

"I don't blame him," Lin says. "Nowhere is safe."

"Empty proth box to our left," G'nar says and sends the image to us. "Let's go."

Lin hangs back but doesn't let go of my hand. "How sturdy is the box?"

"They transport proth across the galaxy safely."

"Good enough for me."

She runs with us into the empty container. G'nar and I put stand with her between us. We're facing the battle going on above our heads. Lin startles with every solid blast hitting the dome. The transparent pieces fly everywhere, bouncing off the Alliance ship's shields before tumbling to the ground. Most land all around the main building we're in. Others fly up before bouncing off of the outside and sliding down the dome.

"Do they know we're here?"

"Yes," I reassure her. "We included a meetup point in our reports." The three of us watch as the Alliance ships pick off the smaller Vahd vessels as they try to outmaneuver the shots.

"Should they be destroying the fuel we worked so hard to mine?" When I look at her, she's frowning. "Thousands of people died to dig for the stuff and if it's so valuable, why doesn't the Alliance use it for themselves?"

"Search for proth use and application within the Alliance members," I say, and her eyes go blank.

"Ah. Makes sense. Too unstable to be practical. The hundreds of disasters while trying to find a safer way to use is awful." Her focus sharpens as she glances at me before going back to viewing the battle outside. "No wonder you were so intent on shutting down all of this."

G'nar mutters, "Never mind the slave labor the Vahdmoshi used. So many of these people can't be repatriated to their home worlds. I don't know which course the Alliance will take with them."

One last proth cargo ship stands empty at the far end of the hangar. I don't move as an Alliance ship drops down, obliterating our view of everything above. Nothing happens for a few moments. For Lin's sake, I tell the two of them, *They're making sure no one's on board.* A sweep of the entire area is done. I feel the signals as a physical touch when they pass over us.

Several times, I've heard Lin begin to ask a question over the innercom before stopping to access her database. The bionans' advanced programming has given her everything I have. I want her independence for her sake but need her dependence on me for mine. I glance down at her while she watches the Alliance ship land. She's perfect, and I want the best of everything the galaxy has to offer for her.

I stop staring at Lin to watch our ship's loading ramp open. Our director comes out with several newly promoted

Protectors behind her. They fan out while Director Tira heads for us.

The ship's engines wind down and sounds of the battle outside bleed into the area. G'nar shakes his head. "We're done."

"Who is she—" Lin begins before saying, "Oh shit. We're done." She turns to me. "Whatever happens, I love you and am your bondmate."

"She won't care," G'nar says as her boot steps echo across the large room. "She's a Leader. They can't be soft."

Director Tira stops in front of us. "So. This is what you two call a covert operation?"

"Not really," I reply.

She looks at G'nar. He shakes his head. "No. We hadn't planned for some of the events here."

"Good. Glad to hear what's supposed to be one of my newest Enforcers tell me he failed to plan."

"I planned, just didn't anticipate a few of the obstacles."

"Like what?" She steps over to Lin. "Like your partner would be too busy playing hide the post with an Earther? Or that you'd be separated and unable to communicate?" She stares at me. "Both of you should have anticipated losing touch with everyone and anyone Alliance related during this mission. We discussed comm blocks and the procedures around them."

Her comment about hiding my dick in Lin continues to enrage me. I want to object about everything, but the director is right. I let myself get distracted by a union when

I should have waited until after the mission. "Ma'am, you're correct. We didn't perform as expected. We should have anticipated some things and worked harder to correct others."

She begins to say something before her mouth snaps shut and her eyes go slightly glassy. Subconsciously, she nods before her vision clears. "Nice. Thank you for telling me what I want to hear. There's a huge pile of dead sixth and seventh worlders all over the place. A hell of a lot of others are dying or traumatized by the massacre. All of this was preventable."

"You don't think the Vahdmoshi had an exit strategy at the least sign of trouble?" G'nar asks and takes a step toward her. "You think we could have stopped how they programmed the securbots to eradicate any living witnesses?"

She looks down at his shoes before staring up into his eyes. "Do not use that tone. Not after all of this mess." She glances at Lin. "The Earther comes with me on my ship. Her illegal bionans need deprogramming."

"And us?" I ask and don't think I want to know the answer.

"I've decided to leave you two here with the mess you've made. Contact me when you've rebuilt everything and terraformed the planet, and I might let you live out your days here."

17

LIN

"No."

The director stops and stares at me. "Pardon? Do you not understand standard Alliance? You're to come with me. Now."

How the woman stayed alive as long as she has with being such an asshole is beyond me. If I were either one of the men, I'd have told her where to go by now. But then, she's not my boss, either. If they were with me at the Super Save, I'm sure they'd be back talking Mike, too. "I think it's you who doesn't understand." I take a step toward her. "Turkh and I are bonded. I wouldn't be alive without him or G'nar."

Her eyes narrow. "Do you know who would be alive if these two hadn't let you distract them? Hundreds."

The number hurts my heart. I resisted getting to know anyone but Turkh and later G'nar because a securbot could take anyone out at any time. Still, they were people, sort of, with lives and dreams beyond here. They didn't deserve their fate.

I walk backward until I'm behind the two men. "Fine. I am the distraction, and I deserve the punishment. Leave me here."

It's a death sentence, Lin. Even now, the area is losing breathable air. Bionans or not, you couldn't last an hour.

Fine, I reply back to Turkh and cross my arms to keep my hands from shaking. "Go on, then, and leave me."

"Hold on." G'nar steps between the director and me. "Tira, stop this. You're angry, rightfully so, but we don't have time to argue this while planetside. Let's at least save as many people as we can, board the ship, and talk from there."

Her face pales under the Gharian bronze sheen. "Of course." She focuses on my waist and nods. "KirKrell, get her to the infirmary. MacKrell and I will coordinate locating survivors." She makes a follow me motion. "Come on. Let's get PAFs distributed before the radiation levels are too high."

Her mention of radiation distracts me from G'nar's last name sounding like the word mackerel. The emotional dampeners stop my laughter but not the worry about radiation poisoning. Turkh's database, mine now, tells me about personal air filters, or PAFs and yeah, radiation because the planet has very little ozone. I walk up the ramp with Turkh, half expecting to see a *Star Wars* character pop out at any moment. While the ship doesn't look like a specific vessel from the movies, it would seem at home there.

We're alone in the hallway, and I ask, "Where is everyone?"

"At their station. Each crewmember has their place."

Sure. Everyone would be at their battle stations or whatever the Gharians call the fighting stances. The surroundings here are so different from the gray and austere hallways of the mining colony. The smooth walls are reddish orange with a black stripe running at an eye-level meant for the Ghar height. Floor lights run along the bottom. When I ask my bionans, it's dim in here because the ship is on land. A dull roar begins as we reach a closed door flanked by two hallways.

"The flight deck is through there. I'll take you in there once we're headed home."

He turns to the left. When I pull up the ship's general schematics, the functionality is to the left, quarters and recreation is to the right. Cargo is underneath as if the vessel has a basement. I didn't see much of the outside for myself, but the entire thing is shaped like a giant metal kite. The information adds that each director has a ship like this. No wonder Tira was upset. She has a lot of responsibility. I'd like to dig in more and learn all about the command structure, but we're at a closed door. "The infirmary already?"

Turkh looks down at me and grins. "You were busy researching, weren't you?"

"I was," I reply as the door opens into a bright and cool

blue-hued room. "I'm sure you're tired of answering my questions."

"Never." He steps forward and brings me with him. "Doc. I have a new patient for you. How much do you know about Earther physiology?"

One of the shortest Gharians I've ever seen steps out from behind a table. "Enough to help her." She tilts her head while staring at my injury. "You've let her bleed all over her hip and leg."

"I didn't *let* her."

"Hmph." She motions at me. "Come here and lie down. Since you don't have nanos, I'll have to run scans the old-fashioned way."

I look at Turkh. *We should tell her.*

"Well, the thing is, she does have nanos."

The doctor stops much like one of those vinyl record screeches, and turns. "What? You gave an Earther nanos?"

"I might have done worse than just nanos. She has bionans from me," Turkh admits, and I have to give him credit. He doesn't do anything but confess openly and without a trace of hesitation. I love how he's militant in caring for me. No one can tell him to do anything less if I need more.

Her jaw stays dropped for a couple of seconds before she closes her mouth and shakes her head. "Can't blame you, really. A wound like that, I would have given a seventh worlder nanos."

I search seventh and try to joke around. "No wonder we've had suspicious tech leaps in human history. You people came down and gave us knowledge. Otherwise, we'd still be playing with sticks and rocks."

She laughs and waves a hand over me. A transparent display pops up showing my organs. "Not us. We can't influence primitive worlds. You have to figure the universe out on your own or not at all." She lifts up her hand and opens her fingers like a flower. A group of red dots expand but keep their roundish formation. "See the red? There's been significant damage. Your bionans are trying hard, but they're not enough to heal you." She waves away my schematic. "You'll need some time in the chamber."

"By myself?" I'm not claustrophobic, but still. The idea of being in a tube in a box in space is a little unnerving. Even after everything else that's gone on in the past couple of months.

"Of course by yourself. No one else can be as injured as you are and still live." She turns to Turkh. "You may leave. From what I've heard, making yourself useful somewhere else might keep you employed."

He crosses his arms. "I don't care. I'll stay."

I want to hug him. Instead, I look at the doctor. "Will it hurt?"

"The chamber? Not at all. You'll be asleep for most of the intense healing."

Turning to Turkh, I put my arms around him, and he hugs me back. "You might as well go and see if you can't get on the director's good side. I'll need a handsome Gharian man to keep me in luxury until I find my own job, you know."

He tilts my chin up until our lips barely touch. "All right, but I'll be back before you wake up." He kisses me for a few moments before breaking off our contact. "I need to go, or I'll end up in the chamber with you."

"Sounds good to me."

The doctor clears her throat. "No, both of you won't fit. Go on, KirKrell. She has some healing to do."

Turkh gives me one more kiss before letting go. "Take good care of her, doc."

After sending some naughty thoughts to me, he gives me a grin and leaves. The doctor shakes her head as soon as the door closes behind them. "He's always been a rascal."

"You've known him a long time?"

"A few sas. Come on, the chamber is this way."

I try to not be jealous. Not of her, of course, but of the extra time she's had with him. The doctor had years while I've had days. She leads me over to a tube similar to the translator one in the large gathering room. In this, a flat surface creates a bed of sorts with a clear plastic pillow and blanket. Both will probably squeak across me when I use them. "I really don't care for these small enclosures."

"But you're not phobic." She opens one end as if it were a mailbox on Earth. "Otherwise, you'd be hyperventilating already."

"No. I'm good. In the last tube I had to be in, the translator just hurt and there was no way to escape."

"Ah, understandable." She waits while I crawl inside. "I'll shut the door now to keep the hyperoxy and meds inside." After closing me in, she says, "If you feel panicked for any reason, kick, and this door will open." She goes to the head of the tube and presses buttons on a keypad. "The other side will, too, but people like to use their feet for some reason."

A fine mist begins surrounding me, cold, so I pull the surprisingly warm plastic blanket over me. I lie on my uninjured side with my head propped up on the pillow. "How long will I be here?"

She doesn't look up from her work. "Not too long. By the time you wake up, your mate will be here and pacing the floor."

I have to smile because I can see him as if he's already here. "When should I go to sleep?"

"Right about now I'd..."

18

LIN

THE LAST THING I REMEMBER, EVERYTHING STOPPED. Now, I hear talking. Am I back on the mining planet, asleep in the fields? I reach out with my innercom, but the words won't form in my mind. Turkh's voice comes across strong. "She's awake." I hear some tapping, too.

"No, no, no, don't tap on the glass. She's not a zoo animal like those eighth worlders."

The doctor fusses and mutters some more while I try to open my eyes. There's a sensation of moving and cool air around me. When I can finally see, I look around. The infirmary is the same, but I'm on the outside of the tube. "How?"

"The bed pulls out of the chamber," she says while Turkh helps me sit up. "Some people like to slide inside for healing. Others like to climb in on their own. I had you pegged as a climber."

I lean against him, grateful for his strength. "I suppose

I am. Are we still on the planet surface? Where's G'nar and the director?"

Turkh holds me close. "We're headed home, and I'm not sure where they are. Knowing them, they're probably fighting somewhere."

He smells so clean, and I relax against him. "How did you get a shower and I'm still filthy?"

"No pain anywhere?" the doctor interrupts.

After thinking for a moment, I answer, "No. Nothing at all." I put a hand on where the wound should be.

"You might have some tenderness."

I'm also still wearing my filthy clothes. Yech. "You didn't need to take off my pajamas?"

"Your pah jah mas? No. Thanks to the chamber they're sanitary." She begins tapping on a tablet of sorts. "KirKrell, take Lin to your quarters and clean her up," the doctor says. She looks up from the screen and smiles at me. "Come back if anything feels painful. This is a small ship, so I'll keep an eye open for you."

"Thank you, doctor." Before I can say any more, Turkh leads me out of the room and down the hall. I want to look around at everything, but he seems to be in a rush. "Is something wrong? Why do we have to hurry?"

"Not much farther." He stops in front of a door until it opens and he pulls me inside. The room is comfortable. Looks like a modern hotel room but with puffier blankets, pillows, and chairs. There's no television or telephone and an open doorway is to our right.

Turk walks backward into what I can tell is a bathroom

while taking me with him. There's a floor-to-ceiling mirror on one side with a shower-like enclosure on the other. The toilet is odd, but hey, it's a toilet, and I'm thrilled to see it.

Our eyes meet in the reflection, and I smile. "So you're rushing me to a washroom? I can't blame you. I must smell horrible and these pajamas?" My shirt is ripped in two places. The pants have worn spots between my thighs, and the fabric at the knees is thin. There's a dirty joke in there, but Turkh is pulling off my shirt. I'd rather think about how to get him naked, too.

He runs his fingertips over my upper arm's damage first, then over my waist. "You're healing very well." His hands flatten over my skin.

I watch what he's doing as he turns us until we're both facing the mirror. The blast I took on my left side isn't noticeable at all. The way the burn hurt, I figured I was scarred at least a little. I've lost a lot of weight, too. There are dark circles under my eyes, and I really need a haircut. "I look horrible. Are you sure you want to bond with me?"

He smiles. "I don't look like an Earther, do I?" He takes off my shirt and nuzzles my neck. "Are you sure you want to bond with me?"

"You're perfect no matter what you look like, Turkh." His light touch tickles as he slides his hands back to undo my bra. "But your appearance does help, though. I couldn't imagine letting someone from Gleet undress me."

He caresses my waist, then my hips, and slides my pants off with my underwear. I step out of both. "Good. Keep it that way."

"Possessive much?" I ask, and he grins while wasting no time in undressing. His cock is ready for me, and I would have liked to have caressed him while removing his pants. I give him a fake pout. "No fair. I wanted to peel your clothes off, too."

"You'll have plenty of chances later. I promise."

I let him lead me back into the shower stall area. "Ooh, a Gharian promise. Now I know I'll get to rip your clothes off with my teeth."

His smile fades as he presses a round, flat button in the wall. "Your bite is that strong?"

A glass partition drops, sealing us in the smaller area. "No, but I can dream." The smaller room fills with steam. "Are we in a sauna? I don't think the heat will help me smell any better."

"Not right away, no." He smooths the now damp hair from my face. "It's a gradual process and gives me a lot of time."

I suspect I already know the answer but ask anyway. "Time for what?"

"This." He kisses me with such a slow thoroughness, my toes curl against the smooth, warm floor. He picks me up, and my legs go around his hips. My arms go around him, too, as we make out in the steam. His body is slick already from the moisture. I caress his perfect skin. When I wonder how Turkh can be less hairy than I am, my search bionans start feeding me information about Ghar's evolution. I turn them off. There probably a way to program them to work in the background while I'm busy.

But with Turkh's erection pressing into my belly and ready to go? Nothing else matters.

He moves and presses me against the wall. After breaking off the kiss, he says, "Part of me wants to take it slow. Make this last the entire trip home."

I wiggle my hips. "I think I know which part is impatient and is going to win."

"You're right."

Turkh holds me still and brings his cock head to my pussy lips. I moan, wishing I had control like I did back in the field. He's teasing me but pushing a little more in then pulling out nearly all the way. The anticipation is excruciating, and I open my eyes to find him looking at me. "Please. I want all of you."

He doesn't say anything as his cock slides in me to the end. I hold on to his shoulders, the muscles hard under my fingertips. He begins a gentle rocking motion, and I slide up and down the wall. His hands cup my ass, squeezing every time he's fully inside me.

"I'm close. The first time," he says with each word punctuated by a thrust.

His multiorgasmic abilities slay me, and I growl, "Give it to me, Turkh. Fill me up." He shoves hard into me and stays while heat blossoms within my body. "Oh, yes. That's what I want."

"Ah, Lin," he gasps. "You're everything. My everything."

I'm close to coming until he eases us to the floor. Before I can protest how I liked things the way they were, he has me on my back. I smile and ask, "Were you getting tired?"

"No." He reaches a hand between us and caresses my spread lips. "I just wanted to feel you take me." His fingertips caress my clit, and my body reacts. He grins when my hips lift up to his for more. "I think I found a good spot to linger." He tickles my already sensitive bud, and I gasp as the pulses begin.

"It's the best place, yes," I agree and reach down between us, too.

"No, you just relax and let go."

I don't listen to him. Instead, I make a V with my hand and press my palm against his stomach. Sliding down, I caress his cock with the side of my fingers. "How about now?"

He nods and closes his eyes. "Good."

Before I can feel any sort of smugness over his reversal, he treats my clit like it's a little blob of clay he can't resist molding. It's too much, and I breathe in deep before I climax. My pussy squeezes him hard, pulsating. Each throb makes me gasp his name. "Come with me. Please, Turkh." As my climax eases, he begins moving faster. My oversensitive clit is forgotten as he braces himself against the floor for the harsh thrusts he's punishing me with. The roughness drives me wild and closer to another orgasm. "I'm close again."

"I know. Almost there." After a few more thrusts, every muscle in his body tenses. "Yes, so good."

His pleasure rolls through me, his cock giving me

everything in him. I open my eyes to see the hot, sexy man pressing against me and I'm gone. He's not moving fast enough anymore, so I lift my hips to him over and over.

"My woman's hungry for more?" he says against my ear. "I'd better give her what she wants."

I don't know how he's still hard, but every inch of him is as he's making love to me. Our emotions are tied, and I can feel how satisfied he is. Yet he's still encouraging another climax from me. He's giving me everything, and one last thrust pushes me over the top. My body starts orgasming so hard I can't breathe at first. I can feel every centimeter of him as he slides in and out. We're so hot and wet together. I can't imagine anything better in the universe than being his mate.

He relaxes only when I do. His eyes are a sparkling black as he says, "See what I mean? We were meant to be bonded."

"Yes. Perfect." I yawn as he sits back on his haunches. He's still grinning like he's found a hidden treasure. "Do we need to be anywhere?" I hold up my fingertips so he can see. "I'm getting pruni— er, wrinkled from all the water."

He stands and pulls me up with him. "No. We have a meeting with the director later, but not until we reach Ghar."

The thought of the director punishing either one of us scares me. I try not to let it show, but my hand trembles as I comb my fingers through my hair. Turkh takes both of my hands in his. "She can't hurt you. No one can."

"But you. Can she hurt you?" He doesn't answer but pushes the button to open the shower. He steps out first, holding my hand to steady me on the smooth floor as I step out, too. "She will, won't she?"

"Tira can try." He scoops up all of our clothes with one hand and opens the bathroom door. "Come on. Let's find something substantial for you to wear."

He opens a dresser and tosses me a towel. It's as thick and soft as the other fabrics in the room look. I wrap it around me and watch him as he dresses. The clothes he puts on are simply cut, a dark gray with gold piping along the seams. A shiny black leather mantle goes over his shoulders. He's slender but muscled, elegant, if a male can be such a thing, and hotter than I think I deserve. As long as he's fine with our bond, I am, too.

I hug the soft towel draped around me and sit on the bed. He's avoiding the discussion about his punishment. I don't blame him. Still, I don't want his life to be ruined because of me. Belatedly, I turn on my search bionans and begin looking up military punishments for Enforcers.

It's not good. Stripped of rank, accounts frozen, exiled. He took a huge risk in even talking to me. My heart hurts over what he's done to keep me alive. "What will you do with my old clothes?"

He's still searching for something to fit me. "Have them washed and returned to you. After that, it's whatever you want to do with them. Keep them as a relic from Earth, wear them once in a while, or even throw them away. I'd recommend selling them as genuine artifacts before destroying them. You'd be set for life."

"Good idea." I watch as he continues to search for clothing in my size. With my information access, I know the rooms come with Alliance uniforms and basic needs provided. Still, this isn't his home any more than a motel would be mine.

He stands with a black shirt and pants and brings them to me. "You'll need to get underwear from a female officer's wardrobe. Shoes, too." He sets them down beside me and kisses my cheek. "When we get home, I'll take you shopping for everything you'll need or want."

"Careful with that particular promise," I say with a smile. "I can be dangerous in a store." He chuckles and watches me dress. I really want a bra and go to retrieve mine. "I can hand wash these, so you don't have to bother anyone."

He sits on the bed and watches me. "Have you searched punitive measures for what I've done, yet?"

"I have." I turn to face him, my underclothes clenched in my hand. "I promise you I will do whatever it takes to keep your punishment to a minimum. Lie, cheat, steal, eat the green slop they fed us down there," I pause and smile when he chuckles. "Whatever it takes. And if the worst happens and you're exiled? I'm going, too, and doing anything and everything to keep your life the same as it is now."

"You can't promise..."

I lean in to kiss him quiet. When he relaxes and begins

to respond, I stop kissing him to say, "I can and I will. You saved my life. Now I need to save yours." He's irresistible, and I kiss him again until a whistle stops us. I frown. "Did you hear that?"

"Yes, it's a priority signal."

As soon as he says the last word, a message over the innercom begins. *All personnel, please report to the command center for a special guest.* I frown at Turkh, and he shrugs. The announcement starts again, and he stands. "Now and do they mean me, too?" He nods, and I need to know, "What will I do about shoes?"

"I can find some foot cover for you to wear temporarily."

Foot cover? He goes to the drawers, fishes around for a second or two, and pulls out a pair of socks. At least I won't be near a special guest barefooted. "Thank you." In no time, my feet are warmer, and I'm following Turkh out of our quarters. "Do you have any idea who our guest is?"

"I have a suspicion and hope I'm wrong. If he's here after the attempt on his life, he's taking a huge risk."

His jaw is set, and the tension flows through to his movements. The hallway seems brighter than earlier, less red and more yellow. Later, when I'm not feeling Turkh's nerves, I need to look up if the lighting changes are a status indicator.

Turkh stops several feet from the command center door. He doesn't look at me. "Whatever happens in there, know that I love you, will protect you and will do anything for your happiness." He takes my hand, still staring at the door.

His palm is slightly sweaty, and I give him a squeeze. "I feel the same way about you. We're mates."

He gives me a glance and a slight smile before stepping forward. I go with him as the automatic doors open. The room is crowded with people. The doctor, G'nar, and the director are all there. Everyone wears a similar uniform to Turkh except one man in the middle of the room. Where they wear gray or black, the tallest man wears white. His edging is gold as is his shoulder mantle. Even in profile, with his lighter bronze skin, metallic-like all the others, and blond hair, he's devastatingly handsome. If I didn't have my everything in Turkh, I'd give the stunner a second glance or more. Probably more.

The dignitary turns to face us and his dark gold eyes narrow. Turkh stops, puts a fist over his heart, and bows his head. "Emperor. It's an honor to be in your presence."

Shitty shit shit! Emperor? I don't know everything about the Alliance, but enough to moonwalk out of here. I'm horrified to be braless and in socks. I think I'm going to cry. My nose stings and I close my eyes to keep tears from forming. After pulling away from Turkh's hand, I mimic his fist over chest salute, complete with bowed head. "An honor, sir."

I hear a little bit of a sexy masculine chuckle and footsteps. As they approach, I open my eyes to see the Emperor standing in front of us. He shakes his head.

"You're not a citizen of the Alliance. There's no need for an homage. A simple greeting will do."

My brain doesn't work. Even the bionans are frozen. He's everything an emperor of the galaxy should be. I glance at Turkh. Ah, but the emperor isn't mine like he is. I need to do what I can for my love, so I smile and turn back to the ruler. "I'm not a citizen yet, but I want to be. How can I make that happen?"

"Ordinarily, being born in the Alliance territories is enough." He glances from me to Turkh. "Humanoids from lesser worlds are Alliance wards and not eligible for citizenship until their planets are promoted. Earth has no single leader, so, you won't be allowed to join from there until they have one voice."

The news hurts my heart. As divided as everyone at home is, the borders, the wars, there's no way I'll live long enough to belong here. Before I can despair, he steps in front of me and gives me his focus. "We've all seen the broadcasts from your planet for a long time. Since they started. But what's it really like? Are all the terrains of the universe on one sphere? How do people choose where to live when there's such variety? Are the animals as friendly or sentient as they appear to be?"

I can't help but smile at his curiosity. He knows little about something I'm a subject matter expert in. "Yes, the planet has an amazing array of landscapes, temperatures, weather, and animals. If you don't like how the air feels, drive, er, go a couple of hundred..."—I search for their word closest to my mile— "nars or so and everything can be different. Our axis is tilted, so we have seasons, extreme ones compared to Ghar. Half of the year where I live, lived, is getting ready for being hot or cold. The plants change, the animals hibernate during the cold times, and everyone wears warmer clothes. Then, when you're used to freezing, the weather and climate change to hot."

I try to remember what all he's asked about and smile. "Some animals are wonderfully friendly. They've been domesticated and need human help to survive. Others are still as wild as ever. We keep the endangered animals in a group of enclosures called a zoo and try to repopulate their species.

He frowns. "Are any of your animals sentient?"

I won't lie, I have to look up "sentient." "Yes. Which is why we make the enclosures as much like their natural homes as possible."

"But it's still a cage."

"Yes."

"Interesting." He looks over at Tira. "Which reminds me, Director LureShell, I have a task I'd like you to see to personally."

"Yes, your Excellency."

He nods at her salute and back to me. I'd prefer he declare Turkh and me united before going on his way. I also want to ask him questions, but with the database the bionans give me, there's no need for impersonal queries. "We love our animals, though we are omnivores, and struggle to be as humane as possible."

"Your planet does seem to struggle with the concept in

general," he says, and before I can react, he continues. "What I'd like to know from both of you, Enforcer KirKrell in particular, is why your union seemed like a good idea during this mission."

"It wasn't a good idea, ever, your excellency," Turkh says.

I look from him to the emperor. No wonder he'd said all that back in the hallway. He was going to push me aside in front of everyone. I have to help. "I agree. We, or I, was there to work and survive day to day. He was there to gather evidence. Nothing more."

"I see. When did you know?"

The emperor's question puzzles me. When I think back to when I first saw Turkh, I have to admit, "I don't remember not being interested in him, and it's as if I've always loved him."

"KirKrell?"

"When I first held her in my arms after she'd been attacked. The match was made and accepted, unwittingly, by her at that moment."

"Hmm." He takes a couple of steps back. "You have bonded?"

Before I can stammer that I'm not sure what he means, Turkh answers for us. "Yes. We have. We're mates for life."

The life thing sort of unnerves me. Sounds awfully permanent, but when I look at him, for life seems like not long enough. He's a handsome man, inside and out. I love him and if I had a choice over being abducted and finding Turkh? I'd choose him every time. "I can't regret leaving

Earth since it means I've met him. Whatever happens is worth his love."

"I must think about your consequences." The emperor stares past and between us, his eyes a little glassy from the internal processing. I can't even become worried from overthinking before he's finished. "An instant bond is something to treasure. As such, my impulse is to pardon you both and return to normal status. I can't do so and remain fair to other transgressors." He glances around at the others. "These two are guilty of several crimes which I will post in information. Their punishment is to be served concurrently." He stares at me for a couple of seconds before saying, "KirKrell Turkh and Lindsey Daniels are to be confined to Ghar for two solar sas. No exceptions." He moves to stand before Turkh. "You will still serve as an Enforcer, but planetside only. You will need a proxy for emergency intersolar and interstellar travel. I expect you to prepare your mate for the citizenship requirements she'll need to meet after two sas are completed."

"I will, your excellency, and thank you. You truly are just."

A grin breaks across the emperor's face, and his eyes twinkle before he grows somber again. "I know. But even I have my limits as to when two people accept their bond." He takes a breath and sighs. "Some things are beyond anyone's control. You two may go. There's no need to stay while I have a discussion with MacKrell G'nar about my decision concerning his transgressions during the mission."

He turns toward G'nar, and I'm so glad we're

dismissed. I glance at Turkh for confirmation, and he grins at me before giving a final salute. I do the same, just in case. Via the innercom, he says, *Let's scram before he changes his mind.*

Great idea.

We leave, and as soon as the door closes behind us, he picks me up and twirls me around. "We've been sentenced!"

I hug him back but don't understand his happiness. "How is house arrest a good thing?"

He gives me a bone-melting kiss before leading me down the hallway to his—our—room. "Because I get to spend it with you."

I love this man. He's crazy, and I have to tell him so. "Look, you're used to traveling the galaxy. How are you going to be happy for two years, or sas, cooped up on a planet?"

We're at our room, and the door opens. He pushes me inside and over to the bed. When he sits, he brings me between his knees and looks up into my eyes. "I don't know how to tell you in mere words what spending the time with you will be like. How I'll treasure every moment. How this gives me a reason to explore Ghar with you. We'll see everything, you'll meet all of my family. I want to give you my world in addition to my love and my life."

I bury my fingers in his dark hair. "Thank you. You were my happiness when I thought all was lost and you saved my life several times. I'm honored to be your mate."

After giving him a kiss on his forehead, I think to ask, *How long will it take us to go home?*

Five days.

Good. I might be tired of making love to you by then, I send before pushing him back on the bed.

You can try.

AUTHOR'S NOTE

Hello and welcome to my universe! *Lin's Challenge* is just the beginning of adventures I have planned for the galaxy's finest of the Intergalactic Alliance. Somehow, these hot sexy alien men find their true loves from Earth. The problem is, as you may have read, Earth is a huge nope for Alliance citizens. It's so much fun overcoming that obstacle and making sure everyone has their very own happily ever after. I so hope you join me on this wonderfully entertaining zip through our part of the universe.

Next up? *Pax's Emperor*. I already know the story is going to be an ugly-cry type. There's a reason Pax meets and beguiles her emperor and a reason why he meets her. There's a link to the book below.

Thank you a thousand percent for taking a chance on my debut book in science fiction romance. Do I have other books published? I do, more than twenty, and in a genre far different than this one. I ran home every day in fifth grade and endured an hour of *Bonanza* to get to the good stuff: *Star Trek*. My love affair with the future never stopped, and I hope you love this book as much as I do.

Am I social? Yes! Please come see me at www. facebook.com/authormarajaye because hardly anyone knows I'm there right now. Hang out at my new website, www.marajaye.com or email me at authormarajaye@yahoo.com with suggestions, comments, or even debates about starship captains and who's the best one.

Finally, if you enjoyed this book, let me and others know by leaving a review. You don't have to spend tons of time on it. Just write something short, sweet, and honest. I vastly appreciate your time and effort in doing so, too.

Thank you so much for coming along on this trip outside our solar system, and don't get comfortable. There are lots more from me to come.

Love!

Mara

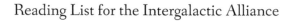

Reading List for the Intergalactic Alliance

Rosa's Abduction ~ The Gharians have been on Earth for a while now! Only available via newsletter signup

Lin's Challenge ~ Lin and Turkh's story set on a hidden mine. Gives new meaning to "dirty sex."

Pax's Emperor ∼ Pax and Eldan's accidental love.

Xell's Entrapment ∼ Xell and G'nar's struggles with a quarantined planet.

Tamera's Fight ∼ Tamera and Dekron's story in a twisted reality show.

Dina's Realm ∼ Dina and Nial's struggles to stay professional.

Sammy's Caress ∼ One Earth woman, one Gharian man, a galaxy of trouble.

Printed in Great Britain
by Amazon